CULT OF THE SERPENTARI

TABOO RITES 1

Book One of an Erotic Fantasy Adventure Novel

{..w/illustrations}

MICAH BLACKLIGHT

A BlackSnow Publication

2022

Cult of the Serpentari: Taboo Rites 1

Story, concepts, internal illustrations, and cover design by
Micah BlackLight.
Copyright © 2015- 2022 Micah BlackLight
ALL RIGHTS RESERVED.

A BlackSnow Book Published by
Whikkid Black Enterprises, LLC
Tolman Creek Rd
Ashland,OR 97520

****ANNOUNCEMENT!!****
Dear reader,
If you find yourself IN LOVE with this story, please do come on over and peruse some of the other wonderful items I have in store: artofmicah.com

DEDICATION

This book is dedicated to the ones who've repeatedly wished more authors would come up with erotica that didn't always involve tentacles, rape, misogyny and the premise that there are no sexy women without giGANTic breasts
[nothing wrong with big boobies, but *EVERY SINGLE TIME?!* sheesh!].

This is for the ones who've wished to see stories where the characters weren't all one color, one build, one race, one anything.

This is for the ones of us who've squeezed our porn for the flimsiest wisp of a story because it tantalized us so much more if there was *some kind* of a narrative accompanying it.

This is for beautiful, fun, exciting, edgy, gorgeously healthy sex and depictions of it. This is for how healing, awe-inspiring and life-changing erotica has the potential to be if we let it.

This is for you, and me, and all of us that yearn for that change. This is because I can't think of a better time to start, or a better place to begin,
than right here

right now.

ACKNOWLEDGMENTS

As with most projects, many factors and persons contributed to this one, some unaware of their contribution, others much more apparent. I simply wish to acknowledge that many such persons will not be included within this list. Whether they know it or not, I am SO grateful for the ways in which they have influenced what you now hold as a reality in your hands.

I would genuinely like to thank Regina Brooks for her role as my agent the first time I went about this (more on that in the Preface), because without her procuring that "book deal", who knows how long it would have taken me to complete my first novel? And I would never have had the pleasure of acquiring a new friend and author-angel in the person of Susan Edwards.

An especially HUGE thank you goes to Susan Edwards, who I think DOES know by now that her support, encouragement, and praise has struck into the core of me like a bolt sent from a crossbow of validation. She's taken pains to make me feel like I, and my work, matter from day one to prescnt day and I am infinitely grateful.

Likewise, I cannot stress enough the deep and abiding gratitude I have for the editing eyes and hard love opinions of Alex Webster Guiney, aka Oysteh Girl, who ultimately grew me as a writer far more quickly and broadly than if I had made this attempt on my own.

I give eternal thanks to my lifemate and partner Opie Snow, for being my first line of defense and for tirelessly putting up with my obsessive creative process.

To M.W. Bennet I feel I owe a lasting debt of unpay-backable gratitude for inspiring me to put my characters and concepts to page soooo many years ago, and being there through every adventure since.

Thanks to Arun Rangathan, Ayo Robinson, Ericka [Lilica] Latimore, Maraya Karena, and Sherri Bell for being my willing beta readers for several of these chapters before they became a book.

I also give especial thanks to those friends who lent me pieces of their essence, quiddity, and identities as well as physiologies to base characters off of.

[Most of you know who you are]

Lastly, I would like to thank every single friend who greeted the news that I was writing a novel of erotic fantasy with gushing enthusiasm and excitement for the finished product. The little reaffirmations along the way sustained and aided me tremendously in overcoming the manifold niggling doubts my internal saboteur would love to have used to paralyze me. I am seriously, sincerely, authentically grateful to every one of you.

PREFACE

Aright so here's the thing.

This is not my first go-round with this particular project. As such, I wanted to take this moment to speak a few words concerning persistence, tenacity, vision, and the willingness to continue on through *valleys* worth of disappointment.

I had, and still have, a dream: a dream of creating beautiful, non-misogynistic, equally arousing and inspiring erotica. And I wanted to get a book deal to do it. With the aid of an agent, I actually got one. It took me two years to write and illustrate this trilogy. During that time, the small publisher I was going with experienced what amounted to a business-breaking series of lawsuits and other unpleasantness that basically resulted in them having precious few resources left to invest in the survival of the company, let alone ME.

By the time I was ready for launch, the most they were ready to offer me was a spot on their website and the ability to get physical copies at cost. That second part was HUGE. I organized two book signings, one on either coast. They were the two best days of my professional writing career to date. Over the course of the next several months, I sold several hundred books. But ultimately, the publisher I was with sank, and though they graciously allowed all my rights to revert back to me, I realized that at the end of it all, getting that book deal had done virtually nothing I'd been taught book deals were FOR.

I'd organized every event I was showcased in. I'd purchased damn near every physical copy sold with my own money. I was the one who asked to be allowed access to the printer in the first place.

There'd been no publicists, no interviews, no book tours.

So here we are NOW. The book you are holding is the product of me recognizing I do not have to buy into the fiction that publishers and book deals are the *only* way I can possibly get to where I wish to go. I am *PROUD* of this piece of work you are holding, and I am determined to continue on this journey.

I've learned so much since I first created this project. I now understand that what I've created is more of an erotic, frolicking road trip through a truly exotic world than a traditional novel. But it's SO MUCH FUNN!!

There is good stuff out there, few and far between as it may be, but hopefully, you'll never have experienced anything quite like what I've created here.

This is the first of much more to come in this series, and more from the other worlds in my head to follow after that. I will endeavor to do the best I can, and hope you remain intrigued enough to continue on with me for the entire ride.

Come get fulfilled. Come be entertained, aroused *and* uplifted. Welcome to the Cult.

LIST OF ILLUSTRATED PLATES

PRONUNCIATION TABLE

-Apachawk: APP-uh-ch-auk
-Atropa Shelale Tarii: ah-TROPE-ah Shay-LA-lay tar-EE
-B-Po: BEE-poe
-Di'aahna: dee-AH-na
-Dhunnoore: duh-NOOR [like moor with an N]
-Domina/Domineh: DOME-ee-nuh/DOME-ee-nay
-Eh'Nas: ay-nAHs
-Ethu: AYE-thoo or alternatively EE-thoo
-Hidatsa: hid-DOT-suh
-Inamorata Liani Tarii: ee-nahm-or-AH-ta lee-AHN-ee tar-EE
-Kithiik: kith-EEK
-Koiya Elizabetha: KOY-uh ee-liss-ah-BAY-ta
-Laquwanda: luh-KWON-duh
-Laliq: lah-LEEK
-Malaas: mal-AHS
-Marchioness Lyssette: mar-key-o-NESS lee-SET
-Marquis Joun: mar-KEY zhoun
-Micipsa: mi-SIP-suh
-Muelim: mway-LEEM
-Naatchri Luunpha: NOT-tree LOON-fah
-Nakia: nuh-KEE-uh
-Nasiya: nuh-SEE-yuh
-Nakoda: nuh-CODE-ah
-Nez: pronounced like "says"
-novishee/novishaarn: no-vi-SHE/no- vi-SHARN
-Osamanche: OH-suh-MAHN-chay
-Ovata Leija Tarii: oh-VAHTA LAY-jha tar-EE
-Raeshe: RAY-shh
-Sa'aeon: sah-EE-ahn
-Sahnish: SAW-nish
-savah: SAH-vah
-savehk: sah-VECK
-Serpentari: ser-pen-TAR-ee

-Shanequwa: shuh-NEE-kwuh
-Shunkerr: shun-KER
-Shawntay: SHON-tay
-Songhai: SONG-eye
-Suush'Wauund: SOOSH-wah-OOnd

-Tabrulec: tab-roo-LEK
-Tamika: tuh-MEE-kuh
-Thauma: th-OW-muh
-twaesting/twaester: t-WASTE-ing/er
-venemaste - VEN-uh-MAHS-tay
-Wabeneyenne: wa-BEEN-eye-IN
-Wah'Ehvi- wah-EH-vee
-Wheirdaahn: weigh-er-DON (roll the r)

INITIATION

Below the sky-ocean but over our heads
The dawn serpents bring us warmth and light
Under the ground well beneath our feet
Gravity 'pents spin to keep us from flight
One serpent descendant is no friend to me
Beware the reach of the Serpentari!

—Nursery rhyme of Wah'Ehvi Towne

One of the most important steps when one is dealing with legends is sifting lies from the truth. When it comes to the Serpentari, this is especially the case. The tales paint them as seducers of men, who'll make gifts of power or steal your children while you sleep. There are more than a score of them or only a frightful pair or just a single one. Beautiful and deceptive, they may even be immortal—no matter the teller, at the end they're always deadly.

But boys' dreams are built upon mens' stories, and if any of the myths are true, a killing will make this boy a man and a legend besides. Closing on his seventeenth summer, his first kill more than two full cycles behind him, Kithiik is strong, driven, and already harsh schooled in the ways of physical violence. His stalwart frame at home on the killing floors of the illicit Tunnel Fights behind the trading bazaar, he considers the veterans his peers, bares his teeth before a match, gives himself utterly to the moment of truth.

Long and short blades are at home in his hands, the result of ceaseless practice and training since he was a squalling brat of four. His physical scars are not the easiest to see, hidden as they are by the deep, rich, ebon tone of his skin; his complexion dark enough to dance along the edges of true black, legacy of his mother. He's watched so many unfledged warriors dream too small, if they venture to dream at all. In order to rise above the masses, to carve a name for himself, he knows he must be willing to risk everything. If desirous of praise, he must do something praiseworthy. Hunting and killing a legend—that is praiseworthy.

Kithiik does not intend to remain in this town his entire life. A need drives him: a profound hunger for the kind of glory that'll land him at the center of the chroniclers' tales, put his name on the lips of young warriors looking to make a name for themselves, and give him a place in history. The Serpentari loom large in his mind; ambition can get you killed, or make you myth.

Unbroken darkness. His torch casts plenty of light and none at all, for anything outside its reach appears inky as a goddess's eyes, and just as inscrutable. The tunnels were created long before Wah'Ehvi Towne was ever founded; nobody seemed to remember what for, or by whom. He's aware that several of the wider tunnels are used daily as shortcut routes by traders and travelers on their way up the mountain passes. More than once, Kithiik has contemplated hiring on as a guard for one of the caravans heading out of the town, if only to visit some of the mountain cities he's heard so much about. But he's got something important to do first, every step in its own time, never a good idea to rush.

If he lives through this ordeal, he'll take his first journey beyond the borders of Wah'Ehvi girded in the absolute conviction of personal initiation; proven as a man grown, fit to stand as a warrior truly. Beyond the rumors and undocumented tales, believable accounts exist if one knows where to look, and who to ask. He's gotten stories from men so drunk they couldn't have lied to save the shorthairs on their neythers. Thieves who've followed would-be victims into one of the forbidden tunnels in the hopes of robbing them blind have instead found themselves transfixed, trying their absolute damnedest not to utter so much as a sound, or even breathe if they can help it. They speak in suddenly sobered whispers about the sibilant slithering of scales against stone, and the screaming; they'll always remember the screaming. Nothing will ever get them to venture back into those crevices again. Period.

This is how he finds himself traversing unlit corridors and high ceilinged, echoing passages funneled through stone; where sound is deceptive, and the feel of moisture in dry air can serve as a signpost. Longblade ready, torch in hand, Kithiik passes deep into the impenetrable black toward his own personal rite of passage.

Many of the passages run parallel to tributaries winding their way beneath the range, and open onto small pools riddling the mountains. The pools leading directly off the Traders' Tunnels serve as watering stops for caravans beginning the trek. Besides the passages adopted by the traders, other paths remain which lead deeper into the base of the mountain. These, either sealed completely, or blocked off and forbidden, are avoided like the plague. Vagrants or bazaar shopkeepers get drunk and then get lost, their bodies later found at the entrances to tunnels people have only recently begun to investigate and explore. That is what dictates whether a tunnel is sealed off or not; warnings like those, silent exhortations to keep away.

He makes his way through the blockaded entrance of just such a tunnel, torch held high, blade ready. Everyone knew who, or rather what, was responsible for the warnings. He isn't the first to go searching for the source in the flesh either. He'd heard tell of a handful of warriors who'd tried it in the past. Unlike the innocents, their bodies were never found. Only two types of people ever go seeking whatever it is that lurks in these Tunnels: the suicidal—those who can't bring themselves to do the deed but don't want to go on living, and the warriors. Kithiik briefly entertains the notion that maybe he is a bit of both, but shrugs the feeling off and keeps moving. He has no idea how long it's going to take to find the hidden weaver at the center of this particular web, and only the vaguest clue as to how he's going to get back again if he survives the encounter. No matter. If he doesn't make it, he'll be beyond caring about such things. If he does, the same will probably still be true, just for entirely different reasons.

Traveling further into the network tunneled through the mountain, at times he finds himself picking his way through rubble that proves to be the remnants of statuary upon closer inspection. The passages he follows seem to twist very little, traveling in relatively straight lines for long distances at a time before turning, as if following a map he has no knowledge of. Several times he passes entire chambers carved from the naked stone just off the passage. In every one, the same savage destruction has made its presence felt. The limited sphere of his torch temporarily illuminates hideously marred, defaced frescos and carvings everywhere. From the glimpses he can see, nothing has been spared, as though the entire network has been subjected to the repeated tantrums of very thorough, very angry children.

Someone went to great pains to reach every available decorated surface, and scarcely an ornamented space on any wall exists that has not been visited by destructive hands. What does it mean?

In no tale that he's heard has anyone spoken of the Serpentari as raging, or crazed. In fact, it was always the opposite. But stories are stories. Nothing is truth but the truth. He has to keep that in mind. He could be hunting a raving lunatic creature and never know it until he shows up on its doorstep, which is exactly what he intends to do.

The chambers themselves look as if at one time, opulence must have reigned within these walls. Despite the devastation, perhaps even because of it, he can intimate the caliber of work lavished on the carvings and crushed detailing. Sunken baths that were probably fed from the tributaries sit empty and deserted, full of the pieces of ruined fountains and their own masonry. Pits in the stonework bespeak the probability of jeweled inlays and the settings for precious stones. Every footstep, every sound he makes feels amplified here; he's never been this deep into one of the forbidden tunnels.

Ultimately, it's the humidity that gives it away—that, and the smell. Tributaries have distinct smells; ponds have their own as well. A mix of minerals, silt, soaked stone, and sometimes, something more. It is the something more that makes them places to be shunned. Gradually the funneled stone mixes with dark green, obsidian crystal, which barely reflects any light back to him, seeming to absorb it instead. The corridor floor beneath his soft leather boots grows more and more smooth, terminating in two shallow stairs before opening onto a large flooded cavern of green crystal and stone. He takes a moment to orient himself, rapidly casting his gaze hither and yon.

She is there. Not fifty feet away from him, a woman floats

at the middle of the pond, only her head visible above the surface. She is not what he expected. When all is said and done, he really has no idea what the Serpentari look like, save only that they are undoubtedly female. But still, he was at least expecting a much stranger physical appearance; something monstrous perhaps, fangs maybe? His torch glitters off the dark, still water's surface, only partially illuminating her. Though he can't see her clearly, she looks like any other woman, save perhaps for the unexpected baldness of her head, mirroring the shaved expanse of his own. She says not a word, only stares at him unblinking.

He takes several steps further toward the bank, notices stairs chiseled into the crystal rock disappearing beneath the surface. She isn't so close that he can make it to her in a leap, but not so far away either. Immediately, he begins to scan the walls for a likely spot to wedge his torch, never taking his eyes too far off her. He takes his time. Whatever the game, he believes himself ready for it. Spotting the perfect place for the torch, he is in the process of wedging it into a crevice when she speaks for the first time, sending shivers through his skin.

"Young…"

He immediately whirls to face her, longblade in hand, crouched and ready. Though she seems to take no conscious notice of his reaction or his blade, he cannot shake the impression that her gaze has missed nothing. In the low light of the torch, he can't even see her eyes, but the feeling is unshakeable for all that. Low voiced, she draws her syllables out slow, a slight, but distinctive accent coloring her words.

"You have come to serve the Serpentari?"

Her speech seems to glide along the surfaces of the rock as if cradled by the walls. Her voice is like a question answering itself, pausing only long enough to trickle through his ears before continuing on its circuit of the cavern. Serve? She just asked if he came to serve. This is something so completely unexpected that Kithiik is struck momentarily dumbfounded. Though extremely careful not to betray his confusion, he suddenly finds himself gripped by a suspicion so intense it borders on paranoia. There are too many possibilities posed by her question, and no time to ponder any of them. Answers will have to come later. *You came here to kill. Keep your mind on the task.*

Slowly he straightens from his crouch and approaches the stairs descending into the pool. The woman continues to stare at him quizzically. He realizes she's retreated further across the pool without his being aware of the fact. Though it doesn't stretch very wide, he can see no way around it. A deeper darkness at the farthest reach of the torch's light suggests another passage on the other side. He'll have to keep her from gaining the exit. At least until he knows more about what he's up against. Every sense alert, every muscle unobtrusively tensed, he sheathes his longblade and warily starts down the stairs, stopping when the water covers his knees. It is warm, but not overly so. He won't have to worry about trying to fight while overheating. Good, that's one less thing to think about. He keeps his eyes on her the entire time. Get her talking. Keep her talking.
"I came to serve."
Upon hearing his words, she smiles a radiant smile, the whole of her face lighting up with something perilously close to rapture. She nods her head, beckoning him forward with her smile. How deep is the water? He wades deeper into the pool, the water level reaching his upper chest as he hits the bottom stair. Perhaps it'll be possible to wade the entire distance. Even so, the longblade won't be an option; a knife job for this one then. He takes a deep breath to steady himself, then ventures further. Several paces away from her he pauses, feigning uncertainty.

"Come", she says. Surreptitiously preparing to draw his blade beneath the water's surface, he takes another step toward her—and finds nothing beneath his foot. He plunges into the water and fights his way to the surface, scrambling backward to a place he can stand. Violently whipping his head from side to side, struggling to clear his eyes of the water, he casts a panicked glance toward the woman. Or, to where the woman should be.

She is there no longer. Quickly he spins, reaching for his blade—and she is there. Standing only half- submerged in front of him. His blades are not. There. Backlit by the torch, it's hard to see her expression, but he can tell she is still smiling. He can see the light glinting off her teeth, and the tips of the spikes protruding from the bottoms of her naked breasts.

Terror.

"Blades will help the little boy not," she says and the smile is suddenly edged with something else.

"Not for this." Her voice itself is edged with something else: sibilant, and low, and harsh, and slow, full of jeering, and the grin that splits her face is like something obscene.

"Or does he fancy himself—a man?"

She whispers this last and cants her head to look at him. He works to stifle the voices gibbering inside his head about finding himself without his blades in a cave with a woman who's not a woman, between him and the only way out. He wills himself to think; to stop visualizing a lonely death no one will so much as mourn in a place he'll probably never be found anyway. Think! Focus. Much closer to the bank than he is, she's exposed from the waist up. His attempt at concentration almost shatters as he abruptly realizes he's never been in the company of a naked woman. *She's not a woman! Don't think of her as a woman! Bone and blade she's got spikes coming out of her breasts!* He looks at her again and forces himself to see. She's shorter than he. Not by much, but still, it's something. He commands his heart to slow; wills himself to focus.

"If man you are," she says, "then die here you will. Right now. If you are boy, you may yet live. Choose."

He finds it hard to concentrate when she's speaking. Knots of fear render his faculties all but useless. Yanking the disparate threads of his thoughts together in a titanic exertion of will, he manages to form the glimmerings of an idea. Not allowing even an opportunity for second-guessing, he tenses his muscles in preparation to lunge—something brushes his ankle below the water. Kithiik spasms and almost forgets about the pit behind him. He manages to catch his balance just in time, but she's closer to him now, gliding the last few feet between them, only stopping when her face is inches from his. He forgets to breathe. Her nipples and the tips of the longest of her spikes graze his chest. Fear makes a statue of him, cycles worth of training spin down into the depths of a subterranean pond in the face of this creature. She emanates an almost palpable aura of something akin to age, and slight amusement, and sex, and death.
Yes, there is death in it as well.

She stares directly into him, isolating his naked fear like a hawk might a vole, her breath cool on his face, slit irised eyes foreign and utterly unreadable save for the dark amusement playing round their edges. She holds him there, pinioned beneath her gaze, slowly bringing a hand up to his chest. He only barely manages not to flinch from her touch as she trails her fingertips lightly down his stomach. Her fingers are dry, though they've been submerged this whole time; her fingernails are s h a r p.

"Does the little boy want his blades still?"

She whispers it, and his breathing catches in his throat. Again. He unsuccessfully tries to keep his eyes from widening. She leans even closer, until her lips brush his with every word she speaks- "What would he do with it, if he had it?"

Her lips are dry too, only of a different quality; like even if she didn't lick them, they'd never dry out completely. Her hand slides further downward, pausing at his belt, slipping beneath it, and continuing on.

"Would he use it?"

Her teeth nip at his lips as she whispers this, fingers finding his fear-shriveled manhood and this time, his breath catches for an altogether different reason.

"Would he?" She strokes his sex, and a wave of shame and revulsion washes over him as he slowly starts to stiffen in spite of himself. Her hand intimately caressing him anywhere is the absolute last thing he'd ever envisioned while dreaming of this encounter. The reality negates his ability to think, to form any sort of a cohesive plan. Debilitating fear and thwarted adrenaline combine to send blood pumping through his system to converge in the place where her palm plays, fondling him beneath the taut fabric of his leggings. Her eyes, still scant inches from his own, emphatic behind the humor in her gaze, dictate his continued stillness through the shameful rising pleasure where her hand meets his flesh, stroking him with expert fingers.

His breathing quickens by increments as he fights a losing battle with his body. His cock grows harder, beginning to throb within her fingers and a smile, small but knowing, blossoms upon her lips, amusement finally making its way from her eyes to the rest of her face. She ups her attentions, squeezing, caressing his phallus teasingly, coaxing reluctant gasps from his throat, making mock of his efforts to the contrary. Her palm becomes more insistent, demanding. She opens her mouth, begins inhaling his breaths as she speeds her pace, subtly breathing him back into himself with every exhale. She is eroding his will, sapping his resistance with the working of her palm and fingers, pulling pleasure from him despite his shame.

He's never been touched.

Breaths turn to gasps and gasps to reluctant groans. His

hands fist at his sides as he struggles not to move them, pinned somewhere in that confusing space between desire and fear, fear and shame. He does not reach forward the few inches it would take to touch her, doesn't know if he'd want to even if it was allowed. But it is not allowed, sees it written like an unspoken law just below the surface of her alien gaze. He's never been touched and this creature is the first and pleasure should not be present here, but his body is responding and his cock is now raging. A release is building and with it comes the fear that it might kill him, the release.

She might kill him the moment it comes. But fear isn't blocking his body's reactions and he can feel the distant building in spite of every one of his wishes to the contrary. His cock pulses several times in rapid succession, his eyes squeeze shut of their own accord at the rising pressure and she stops. They immediately fly back open. Her face still hovers scant inches from his and a powerful fist is tightened into a vise at the base of his shaft, clamping down on the burgeoning roaring waiting there. Holding it at bay, she looks at him askance.

"How would you use it?" she says softly and releases the vise. He lets out the breath he wasn't holding on purpose in a long, ragged exhale. She begins stroking his cock again, slower this time.

"Would you make a game of it?"
She whispers against his lips as he starts to
breathe through his mouth again. "Would
you prolong it?"
Her hand is so expert that he barely notices when one of the spikes scratches the thinnest line across his chest, just enough to draw blood. Not 'til she bends her mouth to suck at the wound does he notice. Staring at him the whole time, her hand continues its business as fire suddenly spreads across his chest, radiating out from her mouth, cold against the heat of his skin.

Gasping, he snaps his head back and feels his body begin to buck like a wild thing. It feels like a betrayal. She doesn't stop licking at his chest even as her hand slows yet again, forestalling the moment of culmination. Without ceasing her movements for even a second, she turns him bodily, pushing him back toward the stairs and the passage.

"Or would you end it quickly?" she asks.

There's blood on her lips. His blood. He's moving like an incredulous mannequin, being driven backward through the water by his phallus and when he stumbles on the stair she allows it to take them to the ground. The stairs digging into his back, the water covering him almost to his chest, he feels sudden pressure at his hips, and is given but an instant to ponder it before he is momentarily overcome with awed disbelief. Throwing his head back, he groans aloud because incredulously, in spite of being mostly underwater, she has clamped her mouth around his cock! In one almost savage movement, she's ripped his leggings open and swallowed him all the way to his balls, sheathing him with the entirety of her mouth.

She holds him that way for a moment, his tip at the back of her throat, his breath at the back of his own. Ever so gradually, she unsheathes him, little by little, pausing at the head of his penis to run her serpentine tongue around it once, twice, before swallowing him a second time. Another groan escapes him and a satisfied purr escapes her as she deliberately takes him back into her mouth, using her lips to savor every inch, stopping only when she can go no further, then slowly rising again. His cock doesn't know what to do with itself.

The tepid warmth of the water keeps washing over him only to be replaced with the heat of her mouth, the writhing of her tongue. Her tongue—the things she's doing with it! Kithiik's eyes roll back in their sockets with sheer visceral pleasure even as he wonders at her feat of not coming up for air. *She's not human*, a little voice reminds him, but he cannot bring himself to care.

He realizes he's begun involuntarily thrusting with his hips, straining to get even further into her mouth, to be wrapped by that tongue. She meets him, matches him, inciting him to increasing fervor. With lips and tongue and hands she works him, urgently licking and sucking up and down the length of his cock. Kithiik moans uncontrollably; arches his back, his mouth wide open. He cannot see because his eyes are squeezed shut; cannot hear for the roaring of his own pulse in his ears. He latches onto whatever meager grip he can get on the moss-covered stairs to either side of him as his body spasms and he tries his best to fuck her mouth.

Abandon like this is completely alien to him. An entire lifetime spent pushing and training, constantly honing his skill and technique has left little time for other pursuits. He's only recently found himself awakening to desires and urges beyond the arenas. Only slowly has the meaning behind certain coy glances been apprehended. His focus has been other where for as long as he can remember. But this—this is something else entirely. This is what the veteran fighters speak of when in the midst of their cups and bragging becomes the theme of an evening. He's unsure he'll even be able to remember it clearly if he survives.

But if die he must, then Gods, let it be this way; gasping for breath while his cock is being swallowed and his body heaves like some wild thing he's got no control over. She sucks him like she's hungry, starving even. He's never been so hard in his life. His breathing is sporadic, and jerky, pulled out of him perforce every time he remembers to exhale. And her *scent*: every time he inhales, he swears he can smell her. An intoxicating, musky, earthy something, a trigger that seems to reach into the back of his brain and turn off everything but the primal. Despite the water and the damp, bursts of it fill his nose, turning everything strange, rendering him animal. Nothing else matters; nothing exists but the blinding desire to fuck, and come, and roar with the savageness of it.

Ultimately he's going to explode, and he knows to his core that this orgasm will dwarf any experience he's ever had. He's braced for the release making its inevitable way toward him, teeth clenched in an admixture of anticipation and dread, eyes screwed so tightly shut he's afraid he's forgotten how to open them, when suddenly, she snatches her mouth away and launches herself up his legs. He groans aloud but does not open his eyes for several heartbeats. He is afraid to open them; afraid of what he might see. He tries not to think too hard about *how* she moved up his body. There is more flesh down there than is natural; more limbs caress him than her two legs. The moment decides itself and all other thought is obliterated from his consciousness. His eyes snap open so wide and so forcefully it almost hurts, his entire body suddenly gone absolutely rigid, bent like a taut bow in reverse because she has taken his cock deep inside her. Simultaneously, both of them pull in a ragged, gasping, sucking breath and hold it. Neither of them moves.

In that instant, he has a chance to see her clearly for the first time. She is atop him, eyes closed, face momentarily glazed in pleasure, and she is glorious. Her body is limned in torchlight, copper toned and sinuous; her medium breasts firm with gold rings through both dark nipples. A darker tattoo spirals back in several directions from her right eye and another adorns her right shoulder. She is gorgeous and alien, powerful, and unknowable. She has no hair to speak of, not even eyelashes. A gold bracelet glints just beneath her opposite shoulder and more gold wraps her wrist nearly to her elbow. It's still hard to see, her lower body beneath the flat lines of her stomach mercifully covered by the water, but he gets a glimpse of strangely colored forearms just before she looks down at him, and smiles a dangerous smile... She is enjoying herself immensely. There's a challenge in her gaze he has no answer for.

Pinioning him with her eyes once more, the brazen smile riding high upon her lips, she begins to undulate. Gently rocking, squeezing his shaft with her inner muscles, she flexes the flesh of her sex as if she's trained it. Irony is in all things. Before he was wrestling his body because it was responding at all. He fights now to prolong the response as far as is humanly possible. Of all the times he's ever not wanted a thing to end, this would be at the very top of that list.

If he'd known what was in store, he'd have tried to hold something in reserve when her lips were all over his cock. Now every single twitch of her cunt drags him a little closer to the precipice. He can't seem to get his jaw to close, taking a breath suddenly requires awesome amounts of control, and every time he does, that infuriating scent is there to meet him. Pushing him to push, hurling him toward the turbulent space inside him he didn't know existed: where sex and sense and satiation are the only laws, the only gods worth worshipping. They urge him to surrender to the beast, the place where control has no place.

His exhales are grunts of animal pleasure; each quiver and subtle shift of her sex sends him closer to crazed. He knows he's lost and no longer cares. She knows what she's doing to him, knows how close he is. He can see it in her grin, the wicked way her teeth clench as she puts a hand to his chest, pushes him back onto the stairs. Slowly sliding up the length of his rigidly pulsing phallus, engorged and throbbing beneath the ponds' waters, she slides just as slowly back down onto it. Taking one of her breasts in her free hand, she squeezes, running that incredible tongue across her lips, watching his face the whole while.

The spasm is her cue, he can't hold on. Apparently she doesn't want him to. Abruptly she shifts tempo. Putting both hands to his chest, she presses down and shoves herself onto his cock, again and again, cunt gripping him fiercely beneath the surface of the pool. Alternating sensations of warm water, warmer flesh, and hot center assault him. She does not slow. Oh gods! She does not tease. There is no game, no artifice. She rides him as if goading him, lashing the beast in him, commanding him to surrender to it utterly, to lose the last vestiges of whatever restraint he has left. He is a scream waiting to happen, a burgeoning explosion that will shatter him into a thousand shards.

When her gasps turn to moans it's a spur as sure as any whip. He's coming, gods help him, and the orgasm itself might kill him. Acutely attuned to the instrument she's made of his body, she raises up at the last instant so that only the head of his cock is inside her. His seed is already in route, rocketing up the inside of his shaft but she hesitates an excruciating second anyway, undulating slowly round the head of his bucking phallus, then grinds down onto him—hard.

Dimly, as if from a distance, he is shocked at the volume of his own utterance. It echoes throughout the cavern sounding more like a death cry than anything else, and for a brief, inexplicably jealous moment, he wonders about the tales of screams coming from these places. Then his body is lost to shuddering and aftershocks and when he finally comes back to himself, she is no longer atop him. He realizes he is laid out at the edge of an underground pool, half submerged with his leggings ripped open. Shakily, he makes his way to his feet, stumbles up the stairs soaking, and completely out of sorts. He hears the sound of cutting air and staggers round in time to see his long blade spinning out of the shadows of the pool. It clangs off the rock wall several feet away from him.

He turns back to the water and she is there, just as she was before. Her head the only thing exposed, floating right at the edge of the torch light; the same, only not the same. He can feel himself consciously editing bits and pieces from his head. What brushed his ankle just before she approached him in the water? He flashes back to the uncanny strength of her hands, the way she felt as she took him into her, extra flesh surrounding his pelvis and how she seemed to glide through the water, never actually swimming, just gliding. Once again, she jolts him out of his reverie, low voice still laced with the slightest of accents: "You came to serve the Serpentari."

It is not a question.

"Yes."

"You have served."

She smiles. Dips her head.

It is a dismissal.

He nods, turns to pick up and sheathe his blade. Gathers his torch to him along with his pride and the pieces of his broken will. Looking back for the final time, he bows low, probably the first time he's every bowed in his life, and leaves the cavern knowing that a great many things have changed. Almost absently, he wonders how long he has before the poison in his chest begins to do its' work, wonders how many have come before him, knowing and unknowing; wonders whether he'll become yet another story, another tale told as part of the legend of the Serpentari…

Chapter Two
FEVER DREAMS

The hero's tales never seem to detail the aftermath. The chroniclers and their audiences revel only in the glorious deeds, the spectacular achievements. What aren't mentioned are some of the inglorious realities: things like stumbling through a half-waking, feverish nightmare with torn leggings and an insurmountable lack of coordination making it impossible to not scrape yourself silly across rock walls with rough finishes. Kithiik is reasonably sure he is dying, and equally unsure he even wants to survive, his entire world has turned inside out in the space of a single experience.

A fever spasm racks him, and he stumbles over another piece of demolished statuary for what feels like the hundredth time. His body keeps shaking, someone continually pounds on an anvil between his eyes and either his blood has caught fire, or his veins are freezing. Body more stubborn by far than its master, his legs continually refuse entreaties to cease moving. Just a little rest and he'll be good as new. Of course he'll be anything but good as new.

Part of him acknowledges this even as the rest of him keeps wishing for peace. Whose body is this anyway, carting him like an unwilling passenger on a ride he can't seem to get off of? That's the trouble with legs these days, he thinks absently, can't get 'em to listen to you. Passing out would be a pleasure, but it might be the last one of his life. Except that before his fever set in, he'd experienced the most piercing pleasure of his entire existence—at the hands of the Serpentari.

That made no sense.

He'd gone there to kill her hadn't he? Wasn't that the whole point: prove his manhood, earn a place in the hero ballads of the chroniclers by killing the legend that lived? But nothing had gone as he'd envisioned. Instead, he'd experienced something monumentally unexpected, and now finds himself literally and figuratively lost. He might also be dead. Wonderful.

Holding his leggings together with one hand, trying to support his weight against the walls while gripping a torch with the other, he struggles to maintain some sort of focus. Better than meditating on what a sorry figure he must make. His only hope lies in holding himself together long enough for someone, anyone, to get him out of these tunnels and into the hands of a really good healer. Sense can come later. Right now, only the next step matters, and the next. Part of him knows he may be beyond help already. Whatever the poison flowing through his veins, it won't be common. No regular herbalist will have knowledge of that which afflicts him.

But he can't deal with the alternative: lying down to die alone in a place he might never be found. So he keeps going. Or at least, he thought that's what he was doing. But the ground feels so good against his back of a sudden. It's cool and dry and a little coarse, but that's okay. He was walking, or stumbling, which, in his condition, is close enough. It's darker. Wait. His torch gutters on the ground all the way on the other side of the corridor. So far away it seems. He must've dropped it. No matter, he won't need the light where he's going.

With more effort than is remotely close to normal, he props himself against a wall of the passage. Wait. Wide. This corridor appears so much wider. This means something. It means…he must somehow have found his way to one of the Trader's Tunnels. Oh good. At least this way, someone will find his body. He'll get a decent burial out of it, and people will know what happened to him, as opposed to never knowing, always wondering. Except, they won't really ever know will they? Nobody could guess how things actually transpired, the reality behind him being here.

He supposes the torn leggings will give them a little pause, make them puzzle over his fate for a while before dragging his body away. Wheirdaahn would kill him—if Kithiik wasn't already dying that is. Teacher, trainer, mentor; the closest thing to a father Kithiik has ever known. How many times has the grizzled warrior warned him away from the Tunnels? He'll be crushed of course, blame himself.

Kithiik doesn't need precognition to see that coming. When Shayla showed up on Wheirdaahn's doorstep all those cycles ago, close on six months pregnant and professing nowhere else to go, it could not have been the most convenient of circumstances for a middle-aged ex-mercenary with an occasional penchant for going too deep into his cups, and a generally irascible disposition. But he took her in anyway; claimed the baby when Shayla died in childbirth three months later; faced down her parents when they'd blamed the child, the man who'd made her pregnant, and even Wheirdaahn for being the sort of friend their wayward daughter felt she could run to in the first place.

He'd weathered all of it, tucked in his jaw, wrangled a small sum for the upkeep of the babe when they wanted nothing to do with it, and let 'em go, raising Kithiik as best he'd known how. Kithiik knows that Shaylas' passing took a chunk of what was left of Wheirdaahn's heart. To hear him tell it, Kithiik was the only good thing to come of the entire situation, bringing a little bit of joy into an otherwise joyless heart.

Now Kithiik lays dying, in the one place Wheirdaahn would've cuffed him unconscious for even thinking too hard about venturing into. He can hear the voice of his mentor now, but of course that's impossible. Though he's not afraid to cross over, he never imagined ending like this, undone without even raising a blade. Let death come to him on a battlefield surrounded by bodies he'd put down, not alone in a gods-forsaken tunnel with a chest full of poison and palsied knees! If not a battlefield, at least let it be on the killing floors of the Tunnel Fights!

A memory flashes to the surface: reciting the creed of the Death Duels for the first time. "We are here to bring death to one who wishes it. We shall hasten them on their way; assure their swift passage with our own hands. One of us crosses over this night. The other will serve as ferryman. This is our way. This is our covenant. May he whose time has come make the journey gracefully."

They'd meant them, those words. The Tunnel Fights may have been illicit, completely unsanctioned by the keepers of law, but they were governed by a code nonetheless. Dying within one of those circles would not have been such a horrible thing; might even have had a bit of honor to it at the end. Picturing the miserable sight he must make, he curses himself vehemently to no avail, nothing graceful about his predicament at the moment, not at all.

If the gods are merciful, he may finally get to see his mother, never got that chance. Of course, the next lands might not be like that at all. Maybe the gods will look upon him with disdain, deny him entrance and instead spit him into some horrid, foul place reserved for those who've failed in life. He'd fit that category of a surety. He's brought grief to the only person he's ever cared about, and failed at the only thing that would have put him on a path to proving once and for all he was worthy of more than pity. And his gods, the Gods of Blade, are not known for their compassion.

Of all the virtues, compassion is probably the furthest from the iron minds of those gods. Giving a warrior a clean death, guiding his hand to keep his last strikes true, this might they grant if one were worthy. Alas, worth could be so hard to prove under some circumstances. Keeping his eyes open is becoming next to impossible, the combined weight of his lids and his shame an almost insurmountable barrier.

Finally, he let's his lids close for what may well be the last time. Taking the deepest breath he can manage, he prepares to horde the remaining dregs of his strength. He doubts he'll make it for more than a day. But if there's even the slightest chance, he will give his everything before willingly crossing over. Sinking into the dark, his last thoughts are a prayer of forgiveness to all those he's failed, and a final prayer to the Gods of Blade, that he be allowed a chance to redeem himself.

Dreams can be strange places.

Kithiik stumbles sideways through layers of exhaustion and fever, unable to tell where he is or what's being done to him. Time stretches meaningless as he meanders through the half-realm; Death not sure it wants to claim him, Life, on a fence of ambivalence. Hours pass, or perhaps only minutes, his body a foreign place populated by strangeness; flesh, dreams, and memories intertwine in ways he does not comprehend, and cannot control. Somewhere he sags against a tunnel wall, taking shallow breaths, intermittently shaking with fever and memories both.

The dry, coarse stone against the skin of his back feels like the first time he landed on the killing floors of the Tunnel Fights. Man he fought had been faster than he'd estimated, dropped him and come in for the cut. He was up quicker than the man could blink, slashing a scar to remember him by into the meat of the man's thigh, winning the First Blood match. He'd looked over to see Wheirdaahn's hard face crease into a harder smile. He dreams that smile curdling on his trainers face as he finds out the abomination Kithiik has committed. *I'm sorry!*

He wanders a hazy place on a crumbling dirt road shared by memories disguised as phantoms. They stir and flit, loosing fleeting images upon him as they brush past: the Fights seen for the first time through the eyes of a mewling baby, his eyes. Addicted to the Fights, Wheirdaahn went religiously, the addition of a hastily adopted, squalling brat to his immediate family not constituting sufficient reason to stay away from them. They became the staple of Kithiiks' education. Like a tool for the instruction of Life, Wheirdaahn used the Fights to teach Kithiik in every arena he could think of, from the judgment of character to lessons in manhood.

Showed him how to reckon the likely skill of a man by his stance and demeanor before a match; taught him about commitment, confidence, and even cowardice; forced him to look at what fear could do to a body by watching the ways different fighters chose to meet moments of truth. Kithiik had been schooled about honor, skill, and the value of training when panic tried to find him; when to abandon honor in the face of one who had none, and so much more.

Now, Kithiik begins to recognize the memory phantoms carrying glimpses of Wheirdaahn, and is careful not to let them brush him as they pass—too much regret contained within them, too many unfulfilled aspirations. Haphazardly constructed, half-transparent rooms have sprouted from the surface of the crumbly road at random. Lurking within are the most vicious recollections, ugly things with malign intent— memories that hurt: learning of his mother's death bringing him into the world; finding out his grandparents wanted nothing to do with him, blamed him even, for the death of their daughter. He silently rails at these uglies as he passes through their abodes- *you're too late!*

What can they possibly visit upon him that he has not already inflicted upon himself? He's never been under any illusions. Forgiveness has no space reserved for him. The only way out would have been to carve a place in history for himself- placing his achievements at the foot of his mothers' grave, spitting them in the face of his grandparents. Instead, he staggers through these rooms half-dead, feeling an extra burden of shame climb onto his already full shoulders. His footsteps grow heavier; somewhere his breathing turns torturous.

He wants to yell but no sounds will come out, only sighs from an expiring body far removed, propped against a wall in a place with solid edges. He is only half there. His flesh cannot fully hold him any more than his dreams can. Hence, the fever propels him onto these crumbling roads, wandering half-conscious, half-dreaming through phantom chambers, slashed at by vengeful memories. Another room looms before him and in a bid to get it over with he barges in at speed, coming face to face with a totally unexpected, hooded female apparition. He blinks dream eyes repeatedly, waiting for her to flit past him, tensing himself for the inevitable pain that will surely follow, but she only stares.

"What are you doing?" she asks him finally, light gray eyes boring into his, probing for truth, alert for falsehoods.

"What do you mean? Which memory are you?"

"I mean are you fighting to live or are you preparing to die?" He can't see her mouth, an extra high collared hood covers all of her face and head save for her eyes, and the wisp of yellowed hair that peeks out from beneath her hood.

"I wish to live", he says, "but I am prepared to die." A snort.

"Men," she remarks just under her breath. When she approaches him, he notices the rest of her for the first time. Strangely garbed to his eyes, she is armored in cloth according to the dictates of some alien culture conjured by his delirium. Augmenting the high-collared hood, a single, plated shoulder-pad encompasses one of her shoulders, tapering to a sharp point,

entirely constructed from richly worked fabrics of brown and gold. At her hips, a wide, ornately worked belt of the same colors but constructed of supple leathers, bisects her luscious waist. Short, corseted leggings laced with thin leather thongs extend downward from the belt to just beneath her knees, partially binding tanned, athletic thighs, and beautifully sculpted calves. She is completely naked between collar and belt; full, exquisite breasts crowned by pert, brown pink nipples brazenly displayed above the feminine, curving lines of her stomach. Nothing covers the trimmed, brown-blonde triangle of her sex. As if the armorers of his delirium purposely wished to discomfit him in his own dream.

Would that women dressed this way outside of dreams, he would probably have paid far more attention to things aside from training all these cycles. The apparition circles him slowly: once, twice, three times, appraising. He waits anxiously; nervous, or flustered, both. Stopping in front of him, she brings a single slender finger toward the scratch bisecting his chest. It is where the spike of the Serpentari opened the thinnest of lines in him before she suckled like a hungry babe and spread fire through his limbs.

As the phantom woman's finger nears his flesh, an unshakeable feeling of foreboding assails him. Chambers long bolted and buried within his psyche suddenly rear toward the surface of his consciousness, pressing at the back of his dream-mind, forcing acknowledgement. He's dying now, there's no need to drag himself back into these subterranean places. He buried the rooms for a reason, he's failed and now it's time to move on. But her finger draws nearer, and his fear trebles.

Convulsively, he recoils from her hand, backing up until he hits the flimsy wood, [is it wood?] of the dreamwall behind him. His near-frenzied gaze finds and holds the gray eyes of the dream woman, and all he reads within them is compassion. They convey so much. *You do not have to carry this. This weight does not serve you.* A part of him rebels, tries to reason its way out, abort this action before it can take hold. "What weights? I have no weights but the ones I deserve. I brought this upon myself. I am fine. FINE!"

But the phantom woman is implacable. Silently entreating without judgment, without reservation, she rings his walls and rebuttals round with simple acceptance; watches them crumble inward beneath it. He is shaking and he doesn't know if it's fever or fear. Somewhere, far away and infinitely close at the same time, a body, his body, hyperventilates.

If he had a blade, he might just attack, see if this apparition would bleed, slash at her until she left him alone. But he isn't alone, and she refuses to leave. Imploring him to lay his massed weights aside, eyes every bit as articulate a cry as the one welling up behind his ribcage in answer, she closes the little gap he's created between them, brings her fingertip to touch a point in the middle of his chest.

Instantly, he reels, struck by an unlocking of compacted emotion so acute, it is crippling. A keystone in his chest splinters, bursting an unknown damn inside him and revealing the roiling, septic mass that waits behind it. He inhales sharply, doubling over and convulsing once before exhaling a savage tide he has no name for. A visceral, emotional deluge comes boiling out of him, abrading the erstwhile indelible layer of shame as it passes and his knees buckle beneath the onslaught.

Yet, even as it departs, ingrained psychological reflexes kick in. A need to hold onto the dissipating strains of his own self-loathing grips him. Desperate, he attempts to cup emotional effluvia in the palms of his minds' eye like drops of precious that must not be allowed to leave. She catches him just as he succumbs to the need, grasping his clawing fingers and splaying them open, calming him, forcing him to let it be. *You no longer need this.*

Once again she speaks without speech, her eyes the only mirrors necessary, the only reflection worth paying attention to. Not until the last of the flood dribbles from their palms does she allow his hands to drop. He shakes still, but all is not as it was before. A weightlessness rests where once dwelt grief, a mostly empty, echoing space where before lay a packed storeroom of suppressed regret, and guilt, and pain. Now he is raw, part wound, part scar tissue, a little bit lost and thoroughly out of sorts.

He feels bereaved of something he shouldn't want, but misses anyway. The wraith waits until he lifts his head to look at her once more before raising a single finger to his chest for the second time. He doesn't react as her finger nears him, weirdly numb and open to whatever comes. This time a little smile gathers at the edges of her eyes, warmth in her gaze.

Let me show you something else, she says without saying anything, and touches her finger to the same point on his chest as before. His eyes close and shining illumination rises behind his eyelids. He stands in yet another room, this one littered with light like fallen branches from an illumined tree, bedecked by spiders weaving delicate threads entirely of concentrated light. The air itself radiates its' own ambience, serving as counterpoint to the burnished ebony presence seated at the center of the chamber, clothed all in white. He does not need to be told who she is. He knows though he's never laid eyes upon her; knows to the core of his being. The room seems to tremble as his knees touch ground before her, laying his bald head in his dead mother's lap like a holy act.

Tears spill unheeded over the chiseled planes of his sculpted face, echoing the features looking down upon him with such compassion, framing the eyes of the willful, impetuous young woman who never got to meet the boy child she brought into the

world. Volumes speak themselves through the palms of the dark
hands atop his head as he finally gives vent to the last of a grief

he's carried since birth. Untold wounds heal themselves as her fingers stroke the tears upon his face, coaxing him to finally release the reproach resting at the innermost crux of his private construction: that he was ultimately the cause of her death; that every day he lives is another testament to her being dead. Love is the only thing offered. No blame, not even sadness; only love, and the wish for him to move on. *This is what I want for you,* she says through her fingers. *This is what I want you to take back with you. It is not yet your time, but know that I am already fiercely proud of my son. I am proud of who you will become. Let this be. Let it be.*

It's his own voice that snatches him back from whatever realm he was wandering. That, and the raw feel of his throat. The revelation of his flesh snaps him back into physical awareness with a vengeance. He exits his dreams to land in sob-wracked skin, direly thirsty, with a heartbeat hammering like the house forge of a nobleman intent on outfitting a private army. Though his body seems a fevered, foreign place still, cheeks wet with sweat and tears for the first time since he was a babe, nonetheless his lips stretch against his teeth into a rictus of a grin.

He isn't dead yet.

A disembodied voice lightly shushes him. Gently, someone with soft hands and a warm scent cradles his head in their lap, dribbles water between his lips. Scrabbling along the edges of consciousness, he receives the liquid like the most rarefied elixir before letting go his tenuous grip and slipping headlong back into his personal abyss. Somehow, he takes the impression of the presence with him back down into the dark, along with the half-heard fragments of a whispered conversation accompanying him part of the way:

"What are you doing?"

"Shhh, I'm helping him heal himself. But my methods may

not be so readily accepted by those with whom we travel, so I've waited until now. You know this boy?"

"Yes. No. A little. Is there…anything I can do? To help?"

"He's already made it through the worst of it I think. But this kind of healing definitely works faster if there is a charge involved. For that we could use your attraction to him. Ahhh, there is no shame in it. He is a beautiful boy, is he not? We are attracted to beautiful things. He need not even know it was you. Are you willing? Here, we'll blindfold him in case he comes too close to the surface of waking. See his eyes? Even now he dreams. That is a good sign."

Fragments that fall apart the deeper he plunges; bits and pieces with no glue to hold them, no wherewithal left to make sense of them.

Effort.

He lets go and tumbles… He stands just outside the room jutting from the road where so many demons have been exorcised, so many weights laid to rest. The chamber is empty of course; he didn't really expect it not to be. Turning a slow circle, he takes a last look around, absorbing all of it, trying to etch the details, however hazy, into his memory.

Halfway through his turn he realizes he's no longer alone in the chamber. The hooded woman stands in a corner, as if waiting for his sight to alight upon her. He stares in grateful stupefaction, astounded at the amount of insight and shifting she has been responsible for within this dreamtime. He has not the vocabulary to express the gratitude he feels for what she's accomplished. Searching for words anyway, a lifetimes' worth of habits thwart him even now, stifling his ability to make a coherent attempt at articulating the depth of his thanks. Giving up, he only hopes that his eyes achieve a fraction of the eloquence of hers a timeless time before; that she can read the debt written within them. That the gods would send such a healer to him in the midst of his darkest time is testament to the fact that all may not be lost. Perhaps there is hope for him yet.

She seems to understand. Another hidden smile crinkles the corners of her eyes behind the mask of her collar. She steps toward him and again, he is suddenly, forcefully reminded of her nakedness, the feminine grace of her lines. He dips his head to stare at the ground, not wishing to sully what feels like a sacred connection. "You're doing infinitely better." She says as she reaches him. "Already you have grown much. Such a dreadful weight to have been carrying all these cycles." As she speaks, she coaxes him to lie down on the sumptuous rug that may or may not have been present mere seconds ago, and takes a position kneeling at his head.

"Who are you?" He whispers the question looking up at her, only half-hoping for a reply, not even completely sure he wants one."

"Perhaps the gods have more love for you than you have perceived. Perhaps I am only an accident. It is unimportant. I am here. Will you close your eyes? I have aided you this far, and whilst your soul was opened to me I noticed another area, a much different sphere where perhaps I can be of assistance. In this temporal place between your dreams and your flesh, things become possible that might be somewhat less possible other where. Will you allow me?"

Kithiik almost laughs at the absurdity of the notion that he would deny this phantom woman anything at all in light of what has just occurred. He answers only with a nod, lying still and closing his eyes. He wonders what place on his chest she'll touch this time, what unknown emotional damns she'll uncover now. He doesn't know if he has any left to discover. He's never felt so emptied, so light, in his lifetime. Still, if anyone could reveal more of the mapped vaults of his psyche, it would be she. Silky fabric passes across his eyes as the healer wraith draws a blindfold about his head. A frisson of alarm, quickly quelled, runs through him as she knots it, and guiding his arms over his head, brings his wrists to rest in her lap, holding them there. She will not hurt him; of this one thing he is certain, if of nothing else in this slightly mad, half-dream world. He becomes aware of a second presence in the room just as a pair of hands tentatively flutters over his chest, the touch light and uncertain. Kithiik goes very still, trying to ferret out clues as to the identity of the second presence, as if his dreams, already well beyond the realm of sense, would send him someone he knows.

As if he'd even be capable of recognizing anyone by touch alone! Combat is all he's allowed himself to know for the whole of his existence. He can tell whether an opponent was academy-trained or alley educated by the way they grapple; can suss out when a choke hold is about to be attempted by a telltale shift in weight and intensity; knows unerringly when to go slack in an opponent's grip to minutely throw off their next attack—but knows absolutely nothing of the soft touch of hesitant fingers. Has no experience whatsoever with goose bumps rising in the wake of a trailing touch, as hesitancy slowly turns into something else.

Maybe the poison has done him a favor of sorts. Without it, he would never have come to be here, lying blindfolded on a plush dream rug while phantom fingers trace patterns across his flesh, outlining the muscles and anointing his scars with the softest of kisses. Hands, soft and unsure, yet gaining in assurance by the moment, lightly cup his face. The unseen second presence breathes the faintest of breaths over his cheek, and across his forehead before releasing a hotter breath across his lips.

The barest whisper of a suppressed sigh presages the feel of lips skimming the corners of his mouth, the gentlest brushing of skin against skin. They tremble as they touch him, as if scarcely containing a visceral excitement. With each kiss, the hands cupping his face grip his cheeks just a little tighter. They too tremble ever so slightly between kisses. Finally, with what feels to Kithiik like something akin to reverence, the unseen lips alight fully upon his, mouth to mouth.

Gently, like he is a fragile something, as if he might break, they begin to caress and explore. His mouth is coaxed open, making way for the tongue which runs across his upper lip, slips past it with restrained impatience, and tentatively twines with his own, beginning a marvelous dance. Thinking himself woefully unprepared, Kithiik at first finds himself awkward and self-conscious. He does not wish to appear as grievously inexperienced as he actually is. But the lips are soft and yielding, the tongue sliding in and coaxing his as if inviting him to play.

Still riddled with uncertainty, but bolstered by the continued caresses, he slowly begins to return the kiss. He is rewarded with a soft murmur of encouragement and approval from the woman at his head, and a small sound of pleasure from the mouth of the one he's presently engaging. With growing eagerness, he proceeds to explore some of the possibilities, allowing his tongue and lips to accept the proffered invitation. As if his response were the only thing lacking, the lone barrier preventing excitement from bursting forth, he feels more so than hears a moan come from deep in the throat of she who kisses him.

The intensity of the kiss trebles, the lips exploring his own become hungry, ardent. Her body presses itself upon him, firmly molding its flesh to his contours. Naked and voluptuous, large breasts crushing themselves against his chest, vulva bearing down upon his burgeoning sex, she tries to be in contact with as much of him as she possibly can at one time. He is giddy with the feel of her; intoxicated by the weight of her breasts and thighs, aroused unimaginably by the texture of her pubic hair;

the almost painful grind of it against his sex.

She keeps his face clasped firmly between her palms while passionately exploring his mouth, teasing his tongue. Wrists still pinioned above his head, he does not struggle, just allows his body to respond with more and more avidity, pressing hardness up against the softness of the body bearing down on him. The unseen presence grunts and releases his face. Writhing atop him, she thrusts her hand down between them, grasping almost frantically for his cock as if it will grant her absolution. He can hear her panting in his ear, down his neck, at his collarbone, her breathing increasingly frenetic.

A short, sharp whoop of triumph leaves her throat the instant she finds what she seeks, rejoicing in her prize. Getting a solid grip, she squeezes until the head of his cock bulges where it exits her hand, blindly straining, hoping to be buried in flesh. Reaching down with her other hand, she runs her fingernails across his balls. He can feel her eyes on him through the blindfold, knows she's watching his face, probably reveling in what she sees.

She adjusts her grip so that a little more of his shaft protrudes from her hand, then leans in, sucking at his tongue, biting and nibbling his lower lip. She keeps squeezing intermittently, harder then softer, working him. Her breath is hot against his lips, his cock throbs between her fingers. Flattening the mounds of her breasts against his chest, she raises her lower body above him, running the head of his cock along the wetness waiting between her pussy lips. Her hand solidly grips his shaft. She slides her cunt above her hand.

His breath leaves him.

She's still massaging. His penis is throbbing terribly but she won't let it all the way in, only slowly slides her pussy over the tip, engulfing it in her nether lips for slow seconds, pushing back until she meets her knuckles, then starting all over again. He tries to heave himself up, further inside, but is continually denied. All the while she squeezes. She tastes of the dip at the hollow of his neck, rubs her nipples across his skin, nether lips across his tip, massages.

Breasts crushed against the smoothness of his dark chest, breathing commingled heat, she tortures the both of them by steadily rocking, sliding, squeezing. At some point, Kithiik realizes both he and the unseen one are moaning into each other's mouths. He, mindlessly trying to push himself all the way into her; she, reveling in not allowing it; rubbing her cunt atop the head of his cock until her juices run down over her knuckles.

She begins sliding the tip back and forth faster, and faster still, her exhalations gradually becoming a continuous mewl of pleasure, growing in intensity and volume. Kithiik almost forgets himself, almost chances yanking his wrists out of the grip of the hooded one at his head, only checking the urge at the last second. His breaths are almost pleas now; he wants to be inside the unseen one's pussy so badly it hurts— literally. Still, her grip on his cock refuses to budge, even when her mewling becomes hoarse panting, and her voice spirals up several octaves. He moans almost as loudly as she does: pleas, curses, and wordless exclamations combining to form an incoherent rant as she comes forcefully atop him, shuddering and convulsing, holding him there even then, forcing him to feel every quiver and constriction of her pussy lips. It is almost enough to send him over the edge. Feeling as if he might burst at any moment, he can't bring himself to stop grunting. Rigid and involuntarily pulsing in her palm, her juices coating the head of his cock and running through the spaces between her fingers, he wonders if the women intend to torture him into some kind of internal discovery. The unseen second releases a satisfied sigh into his ear before sidling downward, traveling toward the straining erection waiting for her. Her nipples trace a winding path along his torso, closely followed by her lips, drawing in goose bump ink, skimming his heaving stomach, slowly releasing the rigorous grip on his straining phallus.

After an interminable time, she brings her ample breasts to rest between his legs; pressing them against his balls like cuddling lovers. He can feel their fleshiness acutely, and he's suddenly aware that within the logic of dreams, he is no longer wearing the leggings he entered this chamber with. Thank the gods! Using her breasts like sensual pillows, she sandwiches his rigid penis between them, kneading and massaging before taking the tip into her mouth. This is the second time since this began that only the head of his cock has been engulfed in the warmth of an orifice. What is her fixation with teasing only the tip?

Nevertheless he finds himself gasping for shorter and shorter breaths as the long awaited orgasm rumbles closer to the surface. Suddenly, the hooded one holding his wrists brings his fingers up to her lips, begins sucking on them one by one, encompassing the entire finger before moving on to the next. She matches her finger sucking to the stroke of the second's breasts and lips upon his phallus. The mouth on his cock becomes more eager.

Her rhythm intensifying, she takes more of him into her mouth with each down stroke. Blade and bone! Penis alternately sheathed between the sensual sandwich of her breasts, and the head licked and suckled with every stroke, his fingers receiving sympathetic attention from the opposite end of his body, Kithiik is propelled into a fevered state of dizzying pleasure. The phantom woman at his head shifts her grip on his wrists.

Continuing to suck on the fingers of his left hand, she takes his right and guides it beneath and between her thighs, settling her sex on his palm for just a moment, allowing him the feel of her wet cunt in his hand. Just after, moist fingers push slightly against his open lips. Welcoming them into his mouth, he tastes her sex. She must have switched her fingers for his palm. Envisioning the lusciousness of the hooded ones' frame, picturing her touching herself, the idea of tasting her sex on her fingers is mind-blowing. While the unseen other licks at the length of his cock like she's been given candy, her breasts become a second cunt stroking him every time his penis leaves her mouth, the hooded one takes his palm from between her legs. Pulling it to her mouth, she licks her juices from it.

The combination sends him plummeting over the edge.

For the second time in his life, he fully expects the strength of an orgasm to kill him. He opens his mouth to emit what he knows will be a cry capable of shattering brick, when his mouth is suddenly filled, completely muffled by the cunt of the hooded one. He finds himself howling into her pussy, for she's crawled forward and planted herself over his face, then leaned further forward to run her tongue round the head of his cock and lick at the cum fountaining out of him.

Two sets of lips and tongues take turns twining round his phallus while he moans into the sex of a gorgeous healer positioned above his face? That's a painting he'd pay to see any day. If only he could step out of himself to witness the spectacle of it! As his heartbeat returns to a semblance of normalcy, he can hear the two of them giggling amongst themselves, playing with his cock between them like an errant, and particularly naughty pet. Yet another memory he'll take with him from this hazy place. If only all fever dreams could transpire so!

"Mmmmm, thank you so much for helping me with that." The sentiment, thickened by desire and dripping with implied promise, is not directed at him. Kithiik can hear the delight in the hooded ones' speech, knows she's smiling as the words leave her lips. He feels the second presence go, he knows not how; one minute she is there, the next, she simply is not. He doesn't quite know how to feel as the first lifts her sex from his face; only just has time to recollect his faculties before she removes the blindfold from his eyes. He stares up into the mostly obscured face of the phantom healer woman now kneeling beside him, the slightest crinkling at the corners of her eyes indicating the size of her smile.

"Congratulations, Kithiik, I think you've just broken your fever."

She does laugh then, a pleasant, genuine sound, coming up and out of her easily. He finds an answering smile adorning his wondering face. He realizes it's not something he does very often; realizes as well that change is in the offing.

"Well done."

"Thank you." He finds he doesn't have to force the words from his mouth; shame has no place here. The woman kneeling alongside him has aided him more than will ever be possible to repay. So many questions suddenly teem within him. Do you exist outside of this place? Are you real? Will I ever see you again? Something in her gaze checks his questions, bids him hold his tongue. He settles for the look of approval in her eyes, for the crinkling that speaks her smile.

"Perhaps." Is all she says in answer to the unspoken; it is enough. It will have to be enough. Slowly she stands. When he attempts to follow he is washed by an unexpected wave of exhaustion and cannot continue the movement.

"You have been through much. Now you need rest, true rest, and when you wake, life will be waiting for you. Do not squander it Kithiik. Do not waste this second chance. Live." With those words, the phantom healer woman turns from him and before she even reaches the wall, fades from his view.

She leaves him lying on the rug, his breast filled with an unfamiliar sensation like nothing he's known and it is with no little amount of surprise that he recognizes and puts a name to it.

The space once occupied by the comingled bulk of his grief, and everlasting shame, has been filled instead with peace. Shrouded in awe, reverently recalling what has just befallen him, he sinks into the deepest of slumbers, dreams the most soothing of dreams…and awakens to his physical body.

"Well, well, well. Looks like somebody is actually gonna make it after all. Gods be praised, I never doubted it for a second."

Chapter Three
CONVALESCENCE

K ithiik awakens to his flesh: weakness, exhaustion, a smidgen of dizziness, slight discomfort from a dozen scrapes, beaded sweat. Bliss. All of it is bliss. Because he is alive, and breathing, every ailment he experiences but a marker, confirmation that he still travels the world of the living. Travels is an apt description as he finds himself moving, or more precisely, being moved. The bonds stretched across his chest, waist and legs preclude any real movement on his part, but the rolling, lumbering gait of the beast he's strapped to more than makes up for it, rocking him from side to side like a slightly jilting cradle. Someone must have washed him, his face at least, because his eyes were mostly caked shut when last he tried to open them. This time, he eases them open slowly, squinting at the light. A radiant pod of Light Serpents illuminates the middle of the sky ocean almost directly above him. He can just make out several of their gargantuan, near-blinding forms through the foliage above him. Foliage? Trees. Forest. He's traveling uphill, on a forested track, strapped to an animal capable of carrying a pack load broad enough to support his entire frame with none of his limbs hanging off the sides.

Rawks. Aside from cows, which make horrible pack animals, rawks are some of the only creatures of their size docile-tempered and cheap of upkeep enough for traders to use on a regular basis. Which probably means one of the trading caravans must've picked him up, fur traders maybe? He could figure out more but the effort of lifting his head even a fraction of an inch is beyond him at the moment. Deciding to let it go, he

starts thinking about how he got from the Tunnels to… wherever
he is now.

He clearly remembers deciding to make his last stand against one of the walls of the Traders' tunnels.

Mayhap that was how he'd been found: some caravan run by a rare merchant with a conscience who'd decided to take pity on the blasted body lying by the wayside.

Not the worst fate by a long shot. Must've been a pretty well to do caravan at that, traveling with a healer capable of dealing with the poison running through him. He'll have to thank whoever it was profusely. After he gets some water. Yes. Water would do nicely—and a meal. He suddenly realizes he's starving. It's another thing he'll begin working on as soon as an opportunity presents itself. At some point, they have to stop, and somebody will come to check on him. In the meantime, he starts to think about his current situation. Odds are the caravan didn't send word back to Wah'Ehvi Towne that they'd found a body.

First of all, the rare caravan indeed could afford to spare a man to run back and inform the gods knew who that some hapless near-corpse had been found in the Tunnels. Second of all, the finding of bodies in the Tunnels was entirely too frequent to warrant any real alarm. Lastly, this particular body, namely him, had actually beaten all the odds and survived. There'll be questions of course. As if on cue, he hears a call to halt come from somewhere in front of him, echoed by other voices on back down the line to some nebulous space behind him. The rawk he's strapped to subsequently plods to a standstill. Almost immediately, a head thrusts itself into his line of vision and he is momentarily completely dumbstruck.

"Oh gods be thanked! He's gonna make it itn't he? Aye knew it the basturd's always been jus' as stubborn as his foster father dontcha know! Knew he was too tough fer a wee bit o' fever ta kill. Now he's outta that coma, it's only a matter of healin' up proper. Don'tchu worry, boy, yer Wheirdaahn is here for ye. And fit ta beat ya bloody though aye am, I figure you've done yerself worse'n I could any day. I know ya hear me, don't trouble yerself ta move. Yer alright now ye are. Yes, that's good, take some water inta ye. Drink slow for cryin' out loud! Drink it slow! You been too long wi'out aye imagine. An quit tryna talk! Yer gonna up and give yerself a tizzy fit. We're stoppin fer the evenin' anyway. Rest. Just rest now. Oye lass, o'er here! Help me get 'em down wouldja?"

Wheirdaahn! Here? Somehow, his stepfather is here, which can only mean one thing really—this must be the Wah'Ehvi House caravan headed up to MaahgTain to get float water for their vintages. He's listened to chroniclers stories of the alpine city's founding since he can remember. MaahgTain: built in the shadow of a floating lake whose waters command such a fortune Wah'Ehvi House has made a killing off of them. Wah'Ehvi Towne was even renamed in honor of the House, now growing so swiftly and bringing so much business in that the town may be considered a proper Province someday.

The House caravans collecting the float water are the only ones Wheirdaahn will sign on for every now and again, the only time he's ever gone for any appreciable amount of time. Kithiik had been planning on asking to accompany him for the first time after he'd accomplished killing the Serpentari. Looks like the Gods of Blade have a sense of humor after all. Not one to argue with truth, Kithiik moves on to the inevitable problem: Wheirdaahn will want to know what happened. This cannot be.

Kithiik is not ready to discuss it with anyone yet, Wheirdaahn in particular. The old warrior has his own reason for hating the Serpentari: a deep-seated, intransigent grudge wedged into the center of the man. Coupled with the fact that she took Kithiik before he ever drew his blade, Wheirdaahn will find intolerable and unforgiveable. Bone and blade but the Serpentari had been so cursed fast! He'd not even felt her snatch his weapons, but she'd assuredly done so, as her return of his long-blade afterward confirmed. He'll probably never see the short blade again.

How to explain any of it? The truth? That was laughable. The truth would go over about as well as slitting his own throat before asking for a tourniquet. His entire life had left him thoroughly unprepared for the most insidious opponent he'd had yet to face—his own flesh. Pain? Pain could be mastered, temporarily at least, dealt with in different ways depending on the situation and the extremity of need. But pleasure? What preparation had he ever been given for something as seemingly benign as pleasure? The memory of her scent will probably stay with him for as long as he lives.

Even now, recovering and weak, the mere thought of her mouth on him, of her *tongue*, sets his pulse and body responding in ways he'd be embarrassed to admit. She is abomination! A creature not even human! Loathed and feared by any who've heard of her kind, yet he'd lay down with her, and worse, he can't even bring himself to regret it.

Fortunately, these thoughts can wait. Wheirdaahn's only questions at the moment concern Kithiik's immediate health and well-being: Is he hungry? Thirsty? Does he have any pain? No one expects anything more from him as Wheirdaahn and a shy young girl maybe a few cycles older than Kithiik lower him to the ground. He recognizes the girl from the Tunnel Fights. She keeps the registry of fighters and organizes the opponents for every bout. He remembers her as quiet, and maybe a little bit shy, but he's never paid much attention to her otherwise. If he makes it through the next several hours, maybe then he can tackle the mystery of how she came to be here.

Accepting the water, he temporarily refuses the offer of food, his stomach so knotted with anticipatory tension he's no longer sure he'll be able to get anything down. He manages to avoid looking Wheirdaahn in the eyes the whole time, deeply happy to be in the old man's presence again, deathly afraid of the inevitable questioning. After making sure he's comfortable, both Wheirdaahn and the girl, Malaas, go about aiding with the set up of camp; Wheirdaahn promising to return once all his duties are seen to. Kithiik spends the remainder of the evening watching, trying to come up with some sort of plan for what he's going to say if and when someone finally decides to ask him what the blazes happened. Surely the entire camp can see his guilt all over him; they're only toying with him before getting to the point.

But as the evening serpent pod finishes its circuit, gliding out of sight over the horizon line and leaving dusk in its immediate wake, no one asks him anything. Relatively small, the camp consists entirely of small to medium-sized tents, the largest of which, the kitchen tent, only holds about seven to eight people at a time. The rawks: large, relatively slow moving bovines resembling a weird cross between a robust variety of cow, and a three horned sheep, serve as the only transport Kithiik can see. He counts maybe twenty people in camp all told. Alongside the camp hands, recognizable by the blue and green livery of Wah'Evi House, he counts at least four guards, rugged, hard looking men of which Wheirdaahn is one. Perhaps seven to eight travelers of varying classes who have to be the paying passengers on this particular caravan make up the last of the camp population.

Renewal Pilgrims.

He wonders how many miles each one of them has traveled

for the privilege of viewing the latest renewal of the cycle up close. From the variety of their dress, he'd guess most of them hail from different Provinces. It used to amaze him whenever he'd see a group of pilgrims congregating in front of the Tunnel Bazaar awaiting the arrival of the next float water caravan on its way up the mountain. He'd generally regarded them as fanatics; religious zealots or just crazy people fixated on watching something that happened every morning, of every day of the year like clockwork, except for during a single season. Just because the Light Serpents went nuts for a month cuz they were busy mating and losing all regularity in the process, didn't mean one needed to climb a gods-forsaken mountain to some plateau in the middle of nowhere to watch them go back to normal and start doing what they'd been doing before hormones turned 'em into spaz cases.

But perhaps there was more to it than that. He's heard so many fabulous stories from grizzled ex-vets to itinerant strangers, about all kinds of wonders they've seen and experienced in the course of their travels. None of the stories have left him with less than a thirst to see it all. Perhaps the Renewal Pilgrims feel the same. What must it be like to travel a huge distance from what you know, and journey to observe something you've never actually witnessed, only heard tales about? For the first time, Kithiik feels a sympathetic twist of yearning. Death had come so close. He doesn't intend to squander his reprieve. What did the healer woman tell him? "Live." She'd said live. He fully intends to do just that.

With that thought foremost, he finds his attention turning almost immediately to the girl, Malaas? He's close to incredulous that he's never paid her any mind before, although outside his training, he's never really paid anything any mind when he actually considers it. Things are different now. Something fundamental has shifted within him, and whatever it is refuses to go back to where it was before. Her skin, though not as dark as his, is the medium brown of polished hardwood. Her hair, full of light brown curls and caught up in a single thick braid, falls to just beneath her shoulders; he can tell it's probably hellishly unruly when let out of the braid, probably stands out around her head like a corona.

She's not garbed in the colors of Wah'Ehvi House, but looks to be serving as aide to a traveling scholar, an old one at that; more than one way to earn a paying place on a caravan, he supposes. She wears simple travel gear, loose, cropped pants under a long sleeved button down shirt cinched just beneath her breasts by a broad leather belt ornamented with several chains. The relatively unadorned clothing she wears cannot entirely conceal the inviting curve of very ripe breasts beneath her blouse, or the fact that her buttocks strain the fabric of her loose travel pants. He wonders what her breasts would feel like around his cock, if she'd use her mouth like the woman in his dream.

The thought alone is enough to send blood flying to his crotch. He has to shift position lest an inopportune tent give away his musings. The fact that he thought it at all feels wildly foreign, shocking him into an internal contemplation of his psyche. Staring inward, he is simultaneously chagrined and reluctantly, perhaps even a little shamefully, delighted to find a strain of something different taking root inside him. Some vague, amorphous thing has resulted from his encounter with the Serpentari, even now reshaping his thoughts and beginning to lead them down paths they would never have ordinarily gone.

In seeking to name it, naughty emerges like a shiny bauble amidst the waters of a stream. It's the only word he can think of befitting the entirely alien thing bubbling to the surface inside him; an errant child, recently taught the delights of sugar cookies, then left alone in a room full of them. Several times Malaas catches his eyes on her and he feels heat fly to his cheeks.

Repeatedly grateful for the exceedingly dark tone of his skin, he's sure she'd see him blushing like some unfledged schoolboy of the academy otherwise. He continually looks away, but can't seem to keep his eyes from coming back to her. For her part, he imagines there is something knowing in her glance; in the almost coquettish way she shyly meets his eyes. There's definitely more than the hint of a smile playing about her full lips isn't there? He's not imagining that; he's almost positive of it. However, he has no idea what to do about it, even if it's not all in his head.

Aside from Malaas, several other women move about the camp, some garbed in House colors, and two or three Pilgrims. Every so often, one of the camp hands will find a moment to flick a more than curious glance his way. It can't be very often they get to see someone dragged from the Tunnels come out of it alive. Though the uniforms of Wah'Ehvi House are generally too loose to allow any real perusal of the forms beneath, he finds himself speculating anyway.

Alerted by the sound of footsteps, he reluctantly pulls his attention from his reveries just as the scholar he remarked before walks up. The rather dour looking old man sports a long gray beard reaching all the way to the middle of his chest, and a pretty good collection of creases and crinkles adorning the pale skin round his eyes. Garbed in the traditional habiliments of the traveling scholar, he takes a seat beside Kithiik unasked, and begins spilling salutations from his lips before his arse hits the ground.

"Hello, might I enjoy the pleasure of your company for a time? I am Shunkerr, a scholar and scribe, a seeker after knowledge, and a lover of maps and literature both. I would be honored to make your acquaintance. By what name are you known?"

Slightly discomfited by the formal language, suddenly

reminded of the precariousness of his current predicament, Kithiik feels himself immediately on-guard and wary. "I am called Kithiik, though I don't know why you'd consider it an honor to be acquainted with the likes of me, sir. I am no one of importance here."

"Ah, I am no sir!" says the old man laughing, conveniently ignoring the rest of Kithiiks' statement, "Please, my name will be more than sufficient. Have no fear of offending me. I am far past the age where such things concern me. In the middle of a royal court, perhaps I might pay more attention to formalities, but out beneath the skocean and surrounded by this magnificent forest, we need not stand on such." Here, he pauses and, still smiling, makes a show of taking a long look around. Sucking in a deep breath, he looks back to Kithiik with what he probably thinks is an inviting smile.

It may even be so, except that Kithiik is so keyed up at the moment, any show of kindness from this complete stranger with his talk of royal courts and formalities has his teeth on edge. He knows the scholar can't help but be curious about what in the name of the Scattered a young man was doing semi-unconscious and half-naked in the middle of a Tunnel, and he's probably working his way into asking. Even if that's the absolute last thing on the old man's mind, Kithiik will go right ahead thinking the opposite until somebody proves otherwise.

"Wonderful evening isn't it?" Shunkerr continues. "It has been a long time since I've been out amidst the trees of a proper forest."

I care not where you've been or how long old man. Not wanting to be baited, but simultaneously not wishing to aggravate a potentially well meaning, but curious personage, Kithiik takes the opening he's been given. "Why has it been so long sir—I mean Shunkerr? You're a scholar, can't you go where you please?" The old man shakes his head.

"Actually, yes, and no. My scholarly pursuits do take me all across the Provinces, and every so often, like here and now, outside of them. However, of late, I have been studying almost exclusively within the confines of one or another of the great cities. They tend to have the most expansive libraries, and I can come by tomes and scrolls very difficult to access otherwise." Although Kithiik is only listening with half an ear, he recognizes that the old man likes to talk, and with that realization a completely different set of reflexes kicks in.

"What are you after that keeps you in big city libraries?" he asks and whether Shunkerr is aware of it or not, he now has Kithiik's full attention. Because as of a single heartbeat ago, Kithiik began viewing the old man the way he would an opponent: sizing him up, probing for weaknesses, looking for openings. In fact, so intent is he upon the expression and visage of the scholar, he registers the precise instant he walks directly into the trap the old man has been setting all this time. Kithiik wasn't the only one looking for weaknesses, searching for an opening. It's in the minute bunching of the old man's jaw muscles, the flaring of his irises, though it seems he carefully schools his face to give close to nothing away. If Kithiik hadn't been looking for it, he wouldn't have seen the triumph register at all. He files the fact away for future use: this fucker is not to be trusted. Of course, at present, all of this is moot, for now will come the bludgeon. The scholar takes the slightest of preparatory breaths; again, a thing so subtle it would go unnoticed except now Kithiik is hyper-alert to everything the old man does, every action, every nuance.

"It is so good that you ask. In point of fact, I was actually hoping that perhaps you could help me. You see, my primary area of study concerns the histories of these mountains we are currently sitting in right now, the region referred to as the Lower TlammaTain. More specifically, I am most interested in texts that give reference to the little known history of an elder race whose impact has largely been expunged or expurgated from the official annals of the Provinces. I am, of course, referring to the Serpentari."

No breath. Suddenly Kithiik finds it incredibly difficult to inhale. His capacity to think has likewise been temporarily suspended. He knows it's written all over his face, knows too that the old man is watching and fully aware of the impact his revelation is having on the unsuspecting young man who thought he was so good at sizing up his opponents. There are lessons within lessons. His mind flashes back to the first time he laid eyes on the Serpentari. "Young" had been the first word out of her mouth. As if she'd been expecting someone different. As if she'd been expecting someone at all. She'd then asked him if he came to serve.

He'd been baffled by that at the time. Pieces begin clicking into place, details, incredibly hazy, become clearer by the minute. What has he gotten himself into the middle of? Struggling to bring his tumbling thoughts under some semblance of control, Kithiik closes his face down, turns to the still smiling visage of Shunkerr and looking him directly in the eye, lets him see the simmering there. He does not know the depth of the trouble he's waded into, but he is acutely aware that he does not like to be manipulated. He glimpses a flash of cunning beneath the smile, as well as recognition before the scholar turns away from him and looks out over the camp. No matter what transpires from here on, the old man has been warned.

"School your expression, my boy. That is the first lesson. Do not so openly wear your emotions upon your countenance. You have nothing to fear from me. I am but a humble messenger. I cannot say the same for everyone else here however." Kithiik observes as the scholar attempts to sow seeds of more doubt within him, playing on his ignorance. The casual way the scholar endeavors to pull upon his strings is infuriating. The old man will probably never know how close he came to being knifed, right there in camp, consequences be damned. However, Kithiik cannot afford to take anything for granted, no matter how suspect the source. The time will come when he is more informed. In the meantime, he must play the spider, watch and wait.

A nature lesson from Wheirdaahn cycles and cycles ago: the two of them were out in the small garden alongside the cottage. Wheirdaahn pulled Kithiik's attention to a flat spider's web spun parallel to the ground maybe two inches above the soil between leaves. He'd pointed until Kithiik was able to make out the relatively large, rather ferocious looking spider in a corner of the web, sitting motionless with banded legs and queer markings on its abdomen. "Spiders are the perfect example of predators wi' impeccable technique."

"Wha's impeckble, Wheir?"

"Naa impeckble, lad, impeccable. It means excellent. Some spiders, the orb weavers an' cobweb spinners in the middle o' fancy webs ye see all strung up of a mornin', those ones have googobs of patience. It'd boggle yer mind ta watch em o'er the course of just a day. They wait, and they watch. Sometimes hours, even whole days'll go by wi'out a single morsel makin its way to their lil' silky doorstep, but they're bothered not atall. They just sit, and watch, and wait. An ultimately, they end up wi' a meal, cuz they're ready no matter how long they've had to wait. They never let their attention waver, ya hear me? Never. Now these ones, these rough lookin funnel web spiders that make their webbies crossways? These ones are even better as an example, cuz they're twice as mean.

"They'll watch and wait, sure as sure, but when their prey comes within spittin distance, they spring so fast it's like watchin a catapult. They don't just wait for the silk to stick their prey, naa, they just use the silk as a sorta tripwire, somethin' to let 'em know dinner's arrived. The second the tripwire is activated they spring! They'll chase the prey, muscle it inta submission if they hafta, bitin it over and over, and they'll not be lettin go once they've got it in their grasp. That is tenacity. That is patience, followed by action. There are times when ya need not be the spider; times when you'll need ta be somethin that doesna' wait at all. But if'n the time calls fer waitin, always remember the spider. Play the spider. And dunna forget to choose which kinna spider yer bein, eh? Ya hear me?"

The situation in reality has not significantly changed, it's just that now, Kithiik has been made aware of a specific opponent. And though the old man makes inference to other nebulous possibilities, it is Shunkerr that Kithiik will keep watch for. Others will either reveal themselves or no, but until the old man brings his agenda clear and into the open, Kithiik will play the spider.

"So I'm to trust you then am I?" he asks, a bit of his temper coloring the words cool. He keeps his eyes on the scholar, staying watchful, vigilant. *You're wily but you think you've got me, so you'll relax the tiniest bit. I'll watch and wait. Don't slip old man. Don't slip.* The scholar looks as if he's about to respond to the coolness in Kithiik's voice when they're both interrupted by an unexpected source. Malaas walks straight up to Kithiik with a bowl in hand. Offering it to him, she ignores Shunkerr completely for the moment.

"I noticed you had not yet taken food, you must be famished. The healer says you probably won't be up and about for another night at least, so I brought it to you." Kithiik is momentarily caught speechless, but is saved having to immediately recover when Malaas turns her attention to Shunkerr. "Hello uncle, it looks like you may want to get a bowl yourself if you're done badgering our guest. The healer is going to want to visit with him shortly anyway." Uncle? Kithiik looks to Shunkerr to see him looking back at Malaas with an unreadable expression. Something passes between them, but of what it consists, Kithiik hasn't the faintest clue. The moment passes and Shunkerr speaks: "Yes of course. Perhaps I should avail myself of some sustenance before there is nothing left of it." He turns his gaze back to Kithiik and there is a promise there, pocketed in the folds of skin at his eyes. *You are not off the hook.*

"We shall speak again. I look forward to hearing your opinion on certain matters. Sometimes, it is a refreshing thing to obtain the viewpoint of someone who's seen things I have not, done things I no longer can. I shall take my leave of you for now. Until next time."

Neither Kithiik nor Malaas says anything as Shunkerr makes his way to the food tent. Kithiik's mind is afire. "Seen things", he'd said. "Done things." He could only be referring to one thing, but how could Shunkerr know? Putting it from his mind for the time being, both he and Malaas wait for the scholar to take his leave. Only once he is out of earshot do they turn to each other. Between one heartbeat and the next, tension charges the air between them. She speaks into the space first, shyly, slightly hesitant, nothing like only moments before when addressing her uncle.

"He's the reason I get to be on this caravan, would cost me a fortune otherwise. I'm thinking about learning to scribe, he's agreed to teach me if I've got an aptitude for it." She takes a breath, continues. "I've watched you, at the Fights. You're really good. I've wanted to tell you before now, but never got the chance. You… always seem so focused. I'm glad you're okay, glad you didn't die."

It occurs to Kithiik that he may only have had a handful of conversations with girls anywhere near his age in the entirety of his lifetime. Most of those were during shopping trips to the Tunnel Bazaars, generally involving haggling, or on the rare occasions when a female warrior would show up at the Fights. It wasn't completely unheard of, just incredibly rare, and they were usually from far away. Sitting here now, trying not to be so damnably self-conscious, so unaccountably nervous for no reason, he has occasion to reflect that he should probably change that. He needs to have more conversations with girls, more conversations period for that matter. He also belatedly realizes that he hasn't yet said anything to the compliments and sentiment she's paid him. Willing his vocal cords to work, he opens his mouth to speak when she preempts him. It looks as if she's weighed her words first, deciding whether or not to voice them aloud.

"Umm, there is something else, another reason you should take food and get your strength back up." As she speaks, both of them notice the small party approaching them: Wheirdaahn accompanied by a woman Kithiik hasn't yet seen. "I'll tell you more after you've spoken to the healer." Favoring him with a quick smile, she rises, heads toward the approaching pair, exchanges a few words and continues on. Dread cuts the thrill of excitement her parting words engender abruptly short. This is it, the moment when the world will come apart.

Wheirdaahn approaches with what can only be the resident healer, and he will take this opportunity to question Kithiik as to what the blazes happened. Kithiik will be forced to lie, right to his face, and watch as Wheirdaahn sees through it, and puts the pieces together for himself, and then the incredulous rage and then the end of the world. This is it. Kithiik surprises himself by offering up a brief prayer of thanks to the Gods of Blade for granting him the opportunity to spend a little more unsullied time in the presence of his mentor and foster-father before dropping the guillotine that will bring the end of all things good. The entire rush of thought must be careening across his face because by way of greeting the first thing Wheirdaahn says to him is: "Ye alright boy? Yer not regressin on us are ye? Yer not running a fever again or summin?"

"No! Naa, actually I'm okay. I'm good. I just haven't eaten anything yet is all. Sorry for scaring you, Wheir, I'm good."

"Ah! Phew! Threw me fer a loop ye almost did! Well then, this is the healer ye get to thank fer bein in the world of the living. It was she that got to ye first, and it's been she takin care o ye ever since. Di'aahna, meet my wayward and hardheaded foster-son Kithiik. Kithiik, meet Di'aahna from some land I've never heard of. She'd like to have a word with ye. I'll be back after. Holler if'n ye need anything and I'll see what I can do. It's good to have ye back. Really and truly it is." And he tromps off leaving a completely discombobulated Kithiik in his wake. Palms slightly shaking, adrenaline racing in the aftermath of a temporarily averted personal apocalypse, he takes a sip of the soup Malaas brought him. The earthy, succulent flavor of mushrooms, herbs, and seasonings fills his mouth and just like that, his body remembers it's ravenous. It's so good! He can't remember the last time he had a meal. "You must be starving. If you'd like, I can come back Kithiik, but I must say, you're looking a lot better than when we found you."

That voice. Eyes widened in chagrin and surprise, he looks up at the smiling face above him and completely freezes, an apology dying on his lips. For the second time in as many hours, he finds it incredibly hard to draw a breath. The minute crinkles at the corners of the intense gray eyes, their equal capacity for compassion and intensity, the wisp of blonde hair falling across her forehead, all look as they would if they were the only part of her face exposed. Unhindered by the hood, the blonde hair falls to her bosom in a lustrous cascade, framing a heart-shaped face. Beyond the tight buttoned blouse she currently wears, he knows what her naked breasts look like; remembers the difference between the color of her nipples and the hair of her pubic thatch; can close his eyes and recall the firmness of the tanned thighs beneath the leggings now covering them. Furthermore, he knows what she feels like when she's wet, what her sex feels like in his palm, what it tastes like.

"Hello, Kithiik." and she laughs, merely giggling at first, holding his gaze with her own, speaking without speech just as in the dreamtime: *Yes I am real, yes that was real, yes I am glad you survived, you have been given another chance and I am so happy I get to greet you, to welcome you to this next phase of your life, welcome back Kithiik. Welcome back!* When an answering smile finally works its way onto his face, she throws her head back and gives voice to the deep belly laugh that seems to bubble up effortlessly from inside her like a living brook, joyously flung out and across the surrounding trees. Camp hands look up from their work upon hearing that laugh, and guards pause in their rounds. It is a brazenly joyous peal of genuine happiness and the celebration inherent in being alive. It takes nothing to recognize that here is a healer truly, through and through. Kithiik simply continues to look up at her incredulously as she laughs and laughs, his thoughts a-racing tumbling down the path laid out for them. The fever dream had been real! From the damn breaking in his chest, to the fantastic orgasmic finish, it had all transpired somehow. And he had the laughing woman standing before him to thank for it. How'd she done it? What kind of thauma did she possess?

But wait, she'd had an unseen second hadn't she? The latter half of his fever dream, when the phantom healer woman held his wrists, there was another presence wasn't there? If the hooded one was this Di'aahna, then who was the other? He had very little to go on, save for the fact that whoever it was would have to be possessed of ample cleavage; the unseen vixen of his delirium had crushed buxom breasts against his chest and eventually his balls, when she sucked him to orgasm. As if reading the direction of his thoughts, Di'aahna's laughter finally tapers into chuckles. She looks briefly down at him, her eyes still sparkling merriment, before pointedly looking elsewhere in the camp.

Following her line of sight, he wanders straight into the purposeful stare of Malaas. She's been waiting for this moment, her gaze alive with a barely suppressed excitement. Even without the smile playing about the edges of her full lips, he'd be able to read the tale from her eyes alone. They fairly dance with electric memories and the promise of more to be made. Blade and bone, whatever trouble he's waded into regarding Shunkerr is more than balanced out by the fantasy he's evidently been deposited smack in the middle of! He cannot believe his fortune. He might have to inquire of Di'aahna about the nature of the deities she worships, because he is sure one of them has to be smiling down upon him at this moment.

"You rest now, get another night's sleep. I know you'll probably have questions. Don't think too much on them just yet. Rest assured there will be time. Once we have made the pilgrimage and observed the renewal, we will remain in the city for a short while, time aplenty for speech. Be patient until then, and regain your strength. I do believe there is a certain someone who intends to tax it repeatedly." She chuckles again as she says this last, then adds, "Ahh, the expression on your face when first you laid eyes on me again! Priceless."

Softly chuckling the whole while, she walks away from him. The darkness of full night is upon the camp by the time she leaves him, the light serpents having long since disappeared beyond the horizon. Camp hands light the torches, hobble the pack animals for the night. Ktihiik takes the opportunity to shovel heaping spoonfuls of the delicious soup into his mouth. A short time thereafter, Wheirdaahn comes up and squats beside the tree where they've propped Kithiik. A spasm of anxiety clenches his innards as Wheirdaahn begins to speak, but once again, his foster father temporarily allays his fears.

"I know yer gonna be wanting another bowl o' that soup. Don't worry your mind. I had Malaas put aside an extra she'll be bringin to ye shortly. I've pulled first watch for the night, for all the good it'll do, so you'll prolly be sleepin by the time I return. We're enterin Ethu territory now, so we won't know if we've pissed anybody off until it's too late anyway. Try to get some sleep. Tomorrahs' gonna be the hardest day trekkin yet; they're tryin to reach the kingdom by mid-eve, so's they can make the observing plateau beyond the city. That's gonna take some hard moving. Now that yer closer to yerself, you'll be able to ride upright, but still, it's gonna tax ye. Healer says you'll be getting yer strength back a lot faster now, but don't go pushin it. Be easy with yerself. I've gotta go, but we'll get some time in once we're at the city. I think yer gonna find you like the place… a lot."

He puts a callused hand atop Kithiik's shaved head and ambles off into the darkness. Kithiik settles himself against the tree trunk, no tent has been provided and that suits him just fine. He's always preferred to sleep in the open whenever he can, beneath the skocean and the night lights of the glimmer fish within it. He can't imagine how large they must be, or how many have to congregate to form glowing shapes big enough to see all the way down here, on the surface. The weather's most always perfect, except for during the brief season of Sa'aeon when everything goes serpent shyte, and the Cloud Kingdoms don't extend this far west so the nights are always clear and the views spectacular.

… This is actually the highest up he's ever been into these mountains, things smell differently, the night's lights appear brighter, sharper, even with the torchlight. It feels good to inhale this air. Every breath smells of nature, and the press of life on all sides of him. Small sounds, traveling outward from the camp, and inward from the wild all round, make their way to his ears, along with the sound of jingling footsteps. Malaas approaches using the torchlight of the surrounding camp to pick her way to him, the chains on her belt gently swaying with every step. Immediately his heart goes hammering like he's done something wrong, or is about to do something wrong. That one might be closer to the truth of it he thinks, and hopes, simultaneously. She carries a second bowl of soup as promised, and he notices the first couple of buttons on her blouse are undone. She says not a word at first but kneels on the ground in front of him, just to the side of his outstretched legs. Reaching across him close enough that her breasts brush his chest and her hair tickles his nose, she puts the bowl down on his opposite side. He closes his eyes, breathing in the sandalwood scent of her hair.

"Are you comfortable, Kithiik?" It's a simple enough question on the outside. Nonetheless his mouth goes dry. Amazing how quickly that can happen. He's had no practice at this kind of thing. What he's got is a dry mouth and a hugely hard cock that would absolutely love for her lips to be upon it once again. She gets directly to the point.

"I didn't let you fuck me in the dreamtime because I wanted you for real. I've never wanted anybody so bad in my life." Her eyes are steady and intense upon him, but her voice trembles as she utters the words, and her hands grip the sides of her leggings so hard the fabric strains. "I want you to bed me like you can only do when you're whole. If not for stumbling upon you in the Tunnels, I may never have gotten up the courage to say these things to you.

"I've never spoken them aloud, but I've watched you, wanted your hands on me, your cock inside me, wanted to see what you tasted like. I had no idea what Di'aahna would do. I still don't know how she did what she did, but I am grateful for it all the same. I will not waste this chance. Whatever gods have chosen to smile upon you I thank a thousand times, and part of my tithe to them, whoever they may be, would be an offering of flesh." She leans in close, brings her lips to brush his the barest fraction, "Will you bed me Kithiik?" Her breath against his mouth, her tongue laps at his lips between words, his eyes close of their own accord as he listens to her words, tastes her breath, feels her tongue on his lips. "You make me want to do things I have never done with a man. I want to look you in your face when you fuck me, when you slide all the way inside me for the very first time."

She moves her lips to his ear, keeping her tone low, her voice breathy, intent, and determined. "Then I want to feel you behind me, inside me so deep I have to bite something to keep from screaming. You've gotta be healthy to give it to me like that, like I've been picturing since the first time I saw you step foot into that arena. Get well soon Kithiik. I'll be waiting. Enjoy your soup."

And she walks away, leaving him every bit as flustered, and turned on, and discombobulated as he's ever been. He's already been warned that the next day's trek will probably prove the most grueling yet, but he has no idea how he's going to get to sleep with the fantasies Malaas has left him prancing round his head like the dervishes one sees when piss drunk and hallucinating. No matter, at the very least, he'll lay without anxiety for a time, the fantasies will keep him company until sleep takes him, or dawn comes, whichever arrives first.

Chapter Four
MAAHG TAIN

Kithiik sits as comfortably as he can on the ground of a small plateau situated higher in these mountains than he has ever been, presiding over a dizzying view only slowly revealing itself in the pre-light of first crossing. It is the eighth morning of the new cycle. He has come to witness a natural occurrence made ritual by man. Seven full days have passed since days became regular again, the most definitive sign of the official ending of Sa'aeon, and the beginning of spring. The shortest of the three seasons, lasting only a single month, Sa'aeon holds the crown for the most chaotic because it is the light serpent's mating season.

During this time, days can no longer be counted upon, snakerise and set become arbitrary things, and keeping any sort of time at all falls entirely to the keepers of the clocks, if you happen to live in a town or city big enough to have one. However, at the beginning of every spring, when the crossings go back to normal, and snakerise and set can be trusted again, pilgrims travel from remote and distant provinces to these mountains. They pay homage to the renewal of the cycle by bearing witness as the Light Serpents once again take up their daily passage between the peaks. Kithiik has never been interested in witnessing the Renewal.

But sitting here now, on ground where countless others have sat, knelt, and stood, awaiting the explosion of light and heat when the serpents sail over the crags above him, he gets a sense of the inherent reverence a moment like this can engender. He looks straight up at the skocean, only really seeing it for the first time. There is an entire ocean up there, miles and miles of water glimmering far above the light of the 'pents, holding court over all things. On either side of the plateau where he sits, rising as if into forever, are three of the five tallest peaks in the mapped lands.

To his immediate right is the Tlamm Hurr, and he knows to the right of it, far to the west of him, lies the third peak, the Tlamm Uute. Though massive, these two peaks are otherwise unremarkable in and of themselves. But the third peak, the Tlamm Rem, makes of this entire range a phenomenon unparalleled except in a handful of places spanning the entirety of the known lands. Getting even the faintest glimpse of its' absolute peak, from however far away, is impossible.

Not for any normal obstruction like clouds, or the mist so common further west, but because of the simple fact that Tlamm Rem is one of those known as the "Supreme Peaks": the only mountains in the known lands possessed of the spectacular attribute of towering to such an altitude that they pierce the sky ocean. As the light of first crossing grows brighter, the dawn pod getting closer to the crags where it will burst over the range, he looks to the highest point he can see of Tlamm Rem.

He tries to get a glimpse of where the titanic waves of the skocean, made so much smaller by distance, perpetually smash themselves upon the stolid and immutable ribs of the ageless stone; he fancies he can just make out the spray and froth. Not for the first time he wonders what keeps all that water from crashing down upon their heads, drowning the world in a deluge of falling sky. He now understands why in some tongues, Tlamm Rem is referred to as the "Drowned Peak". He's never been high enough in these mountains to see what that meant on a visceral level. It is a humbling experience.

His entire notion of heights, and the concept of vast distances has irrevocably shifted. As far up the mountain as the caravan had to travel, he now sits higher still, the alpine kingdom of MaahgTain, and even the floating lake beneath which it sprawls, nestle somewhere below and behind him. That thought alone would have been enough to confound him scant days before, as the kingdom has always been the highest point of his own reckoning. The company trekked hard, stopping only briefly for breaks, to arrive at the gates of MaahgTain by just before snakeset; the caravan would not make it up the treacherous trails after dark. But it had been imperative they get to the kingdom by dark of the seventh day, so they could witness dawn on the eighth.

The number eight is sacred to the light serpents, and thus, the eighth morn after Sa'aeon is always the traditional time of observance. Their company only just made it before dark. Representatives met them at the gates and split the Renewal Pilgrims, Kithiik among them, from the rest of the company, taking them to a place set aside for pilgrims. They were instructed to ready themselves and snatch a few hours rest if they could. A guide would come for them well before snakerise to lead them up to the plateau. Kithiik had ridden the whole way, but was still so exhausted from the trek, he'd passed into sleep almost before he hit the ground. Wheirdaahn shook him awake several hours later, Malaas shoving a bite of bread and some soup into his hands, and the both of them half-walked, half-carried him out to meet their guide up to the plateau. Seeing their guide had snapped the remaining bleariness right out of him. Even in the dark he could tell the guide moved differently than normal men, was taller by a bit and more pale besides.

His motions were more economical somehow, more unconsciously graceful. Kithiik remembered thinking that the coming of daylight in the mountain kingdom would bring revelations in abundance. The moment they've been waiting for arrives, the first bright rays of illumination come spilling over the tops of the peaks. Kithiik closes his eyes for a moment and is immediately reminded of the time during his fever dream when the healer woman, Di'aahna, touched a place on his chest and somehow summoned the spirit of his mother. The sensations he'd experienced were very similar to what assails him now. He'd closed his eyes then too, and light had risen to meet him behind his eyelids.

A similar light seems to be waiting for him now, only this time, the vision that presents itself is not a chamber with a lone woman at its center. Differing images come following one behind another, overlapping in places, as if part of an inter-locking web. They appear and disappear at such speed he is hard pressed to recognize much of what he sees. The first and most powerful image is that of a city unlike any he's ever seen. Towers and spirals seem to super-impose themselves over already extant buildings and walls, like a half-ghost city become semi-solid for a time. At the base of one of the cities' buildings, beneath the overhang of a wooden door, is a weeping, feral woman so distraught Ktihiik's heart nearly breaks to see her. A huge, furred, four-legged beast, yellowish and obliquely patterned stands guard over her. On the other side of the door is a hallway with many rooms where a dark-brown skinned man wearing empty spectacle frames lovingly holds a pregnant, turquoise-colored cat with extraordinarily long black ears. He puts the cat down almost sadly and turns his back on it to walk into one of the rooms, shutting the door behind him. Outside the same building, toward the center of the strange city with the half-ghostly walls, lies a courtyard where strangely beautiful women cavort with serpents and chase the men away, frolicking in sensual ecstasy, an orgy of limbs and bodies intertwined and somehow changing. Transforming into…something else.

Kithiik resurfaces almost abruptly from the depths of the vision leaving its imprint behind his eyelids. Immediately upon opening his eyes, he is shocked at the apparent passage of time. Dawn has long ago come and gone. His body is stiff and slightly sore, and he's missed the spectacle of the renewal completely. Furthermore, of the pilgrims who were surrounding him on the plateau when he closed his eyes, most are no longer present. But there are a few exceptions. Malaas, Wheirdaahn, and Di'aahna all sit comfortably nearby conversing in low tones, sharing fruit and cheese between them. He smiles to see them waiting there, his entire spirit unaccountably lightened, and has yet another moment to reflect upon how few real connections he's fostered in his lifetime. But he has made an admittedly delectable beginning. If close friends are to be had, counting two delicious women among them cannot be a bad thing, especially when one, at least, seems absolutely set on fucking him comatose in the next few days if she has anything at all to say about it. Hanging invisible above it all is the unspoken knowledge that he owes everything to a creature that almost killed him—after stripping him of both his pride, and virginity, in spectacular fashion.

Wheirdaahn is the first to notice Kithiik has rejoined the land of the conscious and gestures to the others. They all rise and approach with smiling faces. "I woulda thought ye was sleeping if you hadna' been sitting upright the entire time. Di'aahna recognized ye as bein in trance or hit with a message or vision or summin. That what happen to ye? You getcher first bonafied vision whilst nappin ye little sod?" Kithiik can't help but grin at the blunt and completely irreverent way his foster father speaks.

"Yaa, Wheir, I think that's exactly what happened. Is stuff like this common? Do people usually get visions and suchlike during the renewal? Is that why so many come?"

"There's a fair number a folk profess to having visions during the observance. Happens often enough to not be too irregular, but it's still not the most common thing either. Never took you for a sensitive, but could be you got some of it in yer blood. Yer ma…" And here Wheirdaahn pauses just a beat before continuing, "She used to show some small signs of it every now and again. Mebbe she passed some down to ye. But come on, tell us bout yer vision before I hafta go check in. I'll have more time later but I've been up here too blasted long fer me own good as it is."

Kithiik explains what he saw the best he can, stumbling most when attempting to convey the way the sprawling city seemed to collide with reality. In the process, he becomes convinced that the spectral city was the focal point upon which all else hinged. When he finishes, all four of them sit in contemplative silence for a moment until Wheirdaahn, exhaling loudly, breaks it.

"No doubt about it, you got a bit o' sensitive in you sure as sure. Can't say I recognize anything from yer vision, but it doesn't sound like summin frivolous to me. Looks like you caught snatches o' something, but, by the Gods of Blade, I've got no clue as to how it all fits together, or what it's supposed to mean. I gotta check in with the foreman and make sure all is as it should be. Meet me at third crossing at the entrance to the pilgrims' space. We got catching up ta do. Feels like an age since I've just sat down and talked with ye, and there's summin I'd like to show ye. In the meantime, I'm sure the ladies here'll take care o' ye jus fine. Seems they've taken a bit of a shine to ye."

A wolfish grin splits his face as he heads toward the path. Stopping just before the bend where he'll pass out of sight, he turns and points to a tree standing hard by the trailhead. "That one'll show you the way down."

Looking from the tree to his finger and back again, all three are startled at the sudden appearance of the same guide who led them up the trail so much earlier that morning. Seeming to materialize from the base of the tree, he unfurls from amongst the bark and surrounding shrubbery like some bizarrely appointed plant that stands and bows to them. Garbed in such a way that any one of them would be hard pressed to tell the division between his skin, his clothing, and the surrounding vegetation, it would have been impossible for them to make out so much as an

intimation of his form amidst the foliage before he moved.

Mouths agape, the trio turn back as a smirking Wheirdaahn continues speaking: "You can ask em' anything you like, he'll tell you whatcha need to know bout the way this place works, and he can direct ye to places where ye can relax. Particularly you, boy, ye need to get yer strength back up. Welcome to MaahgTain."

After that, there's nothing for it but to gather up their mats and follow along behind the guide as he leads them back down to the city, silently marveling at his innate grace, and the way his garb seems to shift subtly as he walks. As they come around a bend in the trail, they encounter a clear view of the city in daylight for the first time. The vista stops them completely in their tracks for several moments of awe- struck contemplation. The kingdom has not been constructed according to any architectural style or set of laws Kithiik has ever born witness to. The main structure seems to have been created according to the dictates of a people intent on having as much outdoor space as it is possible to have within an enclosed city. Beginning with rather modest, one-story edifices with spacious courtyards, and ending up in brilliant, multi-storied towers of glass, stone, vine and living wood, crowned with bulbous, weirdly shaped chambers, the city is built in a gradual sloping arc of height running north to south across the plateau the city was founded upon. Surrounding the city on three sides are walls that look like the forest itself teamed with architects to create enclosures for the kingdom. Entrances are living arches: admixtures of plant, tree, and stonemasonry festooned with vines of bursting color.

On the third side, the plateau falls off sharply in steep cliffs eventually ending in the foothills of the lower Tlamma Tain where Wah'Evi Towne resides in ambitious, burgeoning growth. The tallest of the twisting towers line the cliffs where the plateau ends, bulbous chambers at their peaks dominated by massive, many-paned, fluidly shaped windows of etched glass with gilded frames. Thrusting their delicate, seemingly convoluted way up from the forest floor like the yearning fingers of an ancient creature with elegant fingertips, the towers seem to reach toward the greatest marvel of them all.

Holding fantastic court perhaps half a hundred yards above, its waters casting scintillating shadows over a third of the mountain city, hangs the utterly inexplicable, totally mystifying vastness of the floating lake called the MaahgThairn. He's heard tales of the floating lake his entire life; indeed, the founding of MaahgTain has been one of his favorite legends since he was a boy, but seeing the object of the stories in front of him, real as the serpent's light shining through the floating shallows, is an altogether different thing. Buoyed and excited by the idea of exploring this city for any length of time at all, the trio continues down the mountain behind the guide at a slightly faster pace, huge grins stretching their faces like schoolchildren presented with the prospect of a week-long holiday. Once at the bottom, at a fork in the path separating the trails leading into the kingdom proper and the place set aside for Renewal Pilgrims, the guide stops and turns to them. They take this moment to scrutinize him up close like skocean gazers with their telescopes in the academies.

Tall and exceedingly pale, with the fabled alabaster skin, pronounced cheekbones, full lips, and markedly slanted almond eyes that are the hallmarks of his people, his features are angular and sharply bewitching beneath his mottled garb. Kithiik gets an impression of slimness though he can't tell for sure as the clothing effectively distorts his silhouette. Sundry plant-life and other flora riddle his clothing, cunningly attached to the cloth in organic patterns that perfectly mimic the surrounding forest vegetation. When the Ethu speaks, his voice sounds like an exquisitely modulated, quietly tonal instrument that renders the common tongue exotic and full of unspoken secrets.

"You are about to enter into the kingdom proper. Ours is a kingdom beholden to none. Therefore our ways are not necessarily your ways; our customs are not your customs. If you are to enter, perhaps you should consider leaving your judgments at the thresholds of our borders. Ours is a very free way, an open, sensual way; we suggest that guests take their visits as an opportunity to explore different ways of being. If you have questions, ask of anyone you encounter. You may receive answers; you may receive questions in return. Make of your visit an experience you may take with you on your travels. Welcome to Maahg'Tain." After bidding them welcome and leading them to the pilgrim's quarters, their guide leaves them to make their own way. The trek the preceding night was so rigorous, none of them has taken time to wash up since they've arrived, so that's the place they agree to start. The minute they enter the pilgrims' quarters, a long, rectangular barracks with palettes lining the walls, the first thing they notice is the absence of all the other pilgrims save one snoring old woman on a palette mid-way through the hall. At the far end of the barracks is the entrance to a small antechamber, which reveals itself upon further inspection to be furnished
with buckets, tubs, brushes, and various soaps for washing.

Beyond these sits a small hot spring that could be used to fill the tubs, or just for refreshment. Although he searches, Kithiik can see no separated space, no curtains, dividers or anything designating where the women should bathe verses the males. Not wanting to ruin what could turn out to be a very interesting potential, he says nothing but makes his way to the palette he slept in before realizing he has absolutely no belongings that aren't already on him.

Come to think of it, he doesn't even know whose clothes he's wearing. His tryst with the Serpentari ruined his own leggings, and when he awoke, he found himself wearing someone else's. He's got no money on him at all, and no real recourse. What he's got on will have to suffice until he gets back to Wah'Evi Towne. He looks up to see Malaas and Di'aahna waiting for him at the entrance to the antechamber.

"You coming or what?" says Di'aahna with a mischievous smile and a toss of her blonde head. "We have to get cleaned up and I don't know about you, but I didn't see any dividers anywhere. Did you Malaas?"

"No, I didn't see anything of the sort. It seems that uncle's gone on up ahead to explore, and Wheirdaahn's busy checking in. You've gotta get your strength back up Kithiik and we have been charged with making sure you do. So…" Unable to keep a smile from breaking out on his face, his penis surging in anticipation, Kithiik tries his best not to run the distance from his palette to the antechamber. Closing the doors behind him, Kithiik busies himself filling one of the tubs from the spring while the women begin to strip off their clothes.

"I don't know if I'm going to take a full bath this time Kithiik," Di'aahna says while stripping off the last of her clothes, "so maybe instead of filling up the tub you could help me? Maybe you could scrub my back while she scrubs yours, and I can scrub hers."

Swallowing, he starts toward Di'aahna, grabbing a bucket as he passes, when Malaas looks at him and asks, "Aren't you forgetting something Kithiik?" arching an eyebrow at his clothes. He's forgotten to take them off. For the billionth time, he offers up a prayer of thanks for the darkness of his skin; surely, they'd see him blushing terribly without it.

"Maybe he needs a little help." D'aahna says teasingly. "Do you need us to come help you Kithiik? We know you've been through a lot."

And she laughs that laugh again, with Malaas joining in, and Kithiik, mumbling something about not needing any help, thoroughly embarrassed at himself, fumbles off his clothes and makes his way over to the women. They take turns dousing each other with the pails, the girls giggling the whole time and then Di'aahna picks up a chunk of soap.

"So," she asks innocently, "who gets lathered first?"

Still unable to believe the immensity of his good fortune, Kithiik takes the opportunity to try out some of the privileges he's apparently been awarded. "I nominate you" he says, and turns to see Malaas nodding her head in approval while reaching for her own clump of soap.

"With pleasure" Di'aahna answers, handing her chunk of soap over. Taking it from her, he turns her around and begins to lather her naked body, choosing to start from her ankles and work his way up. Malaas, taking her cue from him, begins at the same place, only from the front. She faces him through Di'aahna's legs, eyes smoldering with gleeful promise and anticipation. They make their way up her form, Kithiik rounding the curves of her calves, absolutely stupefied that he gets a chance to go over every inch of her luscious frame in this way, tanned and toned and gorgeous as it is.

His hand trails behind the soap, massaging and lathering, following

every contour and nuance of her legs, working his way upward past her knees to her delicious thighs. He knows what her body looks like from his fever dream, but to revel in it like this is heaven. He runs his hand over her

73

buttocks before taking the chunk up the crack of her ass. Malaas catches his eyes from Di'aahna's other side. Looking wicked in a way Kithiik has not yet seen, she deliberately runs her soap along the slit between Di'aahna's legs. Both feel her judder in response. Kithiik rises, running the soap up Di'aahna's spine as he does so, is in the process of lathing it across her shoulders when she leans back into him. Her head falling back onto his shoulder, lips slightly parted, she stares into Malaas' eyes and he realizes what is happening. Malaas hasn't taken her hand from between Di'aahna's legs. She's slicked her pussy lips with the soap and her fingers are busy down there.

Kithiik can't believe what he's seeing. Going from virgin to this is ridiculous. He's never even heard of such things happening. Now he's living them on an almost daily basis. Judging by the look on Malaas's face, she's almost as surprised as he is. A mixture of desire, curiosity, and what looks a little bit like burgeoning triumph take turns playing along her features. The girls' gazes are locked on each other, Malaas increasing her pace incrementally as Di'aahna begins to pant softly. Kithiik drops the clump, takes his soapy hands and runs them all over her torso, reveling in the freedom of it. Until several days ago, he'd never so much as touched or even seen a naked woman before.

Now, his hands meander around the naked, soapy sides of a gorgeous woman and up to her perfectly pert breasts. He cups them in his hands, feeling the shape and weight of them, before running his palms across her nipples. Though he knows it not, his expression is quite close to mirroring that of Malaas. Di'aahna tears her gaze from Malaas, grabs the back of Kithiik's neck and yanks his head down to meet her own. She kisses him hungrily, tongue pushing into his mouth, running rampant round his teeth. He grabs hold of her breasts and squeezes, pulling her back into him. Her ass presses into his crotch, and he grinds himself against the soapy slickness of it, cock sliding between her cheeks, involuntarily triggering carnal thoughts he's never entertained before. What would *that* feel like?

She lets go of his neck, pulls her face away and is immediately met by Malaas. The two of them explore each other's mouths in front of him, lips and tongues busily engaged. Tentatively, he brings his lips to her neck, nuzzles her while she kisses Malaas; finds that he likes biting her softly, and maybe not so softly. Her breathing is growing more strenuous, her hips jerking faster in time to the ministrations of Malaas' fingers, when they all hear someone come into the barracks, on the far side of the hall from the antechamber door. Kithiik gets an idea.

Bending his knees, he crouches so that the head of his penis is pushing slightly against Malaas' fingers working in Di'aahna's cunt. Malaas takes the cue and doubles her efforts, bringing Di'aahna to the knife's edge of coming before snatching her fingers away. The minute her fingers pull out, Kithiik buries himself inside her wetness up to his balls, instantly sending Di'aahna exploding over the edge. She throws her head back to Kithiik's shoulder once more, leaning into him, using his weight as leverage while her pelvis rocks uncontrollably against the cock driving her across the threshold of orgasm.

Kithiik clamps his hand over her open mouth, her pants pumping into his palm like smothered barks of release as her body quakes in his grip. He clenches his teeth against his own grunts of pleasure and holds her like that until she collapses against him. It is an effort of will to pull out of her, but he does so on wobbly knees, letting her tumble into Malaas's arms; a mess of limbs and hair and gasping woman, temporarily unable to support her own weight in the aftermath of orgasm.

The movement on the other side of the door hasn't stopped. The old woman's snoring has. They can hear her speaking sleepily with whoever entered the room. It sounds like Shunkerr. Grinning like wayward schoolchildren, the three of them head to separate washing troughs, Di'aahna slowly regaining control of her breathing, still being hit by aftershocks. Malaas notices Kithiik's continued hardness and almost leaves her washing trough when all three of them hear the footsteps approaching the door to the antechamber. Promptly dumping water all over herself, Malaas lathers and speaks into the silence at the same time: "Oh, this is just what I've been wanting, I feel like I haven't washed in way too long."

"I know it's exactly what I needed." Di'aahna answers, her voice only slightly trembling. Kithiik says nothing, only proceeds to wash and rinse as quickly as he can, trying to quiet the raging of his unsated cock. Grabbing his clothes, he tip toes to the hot spring, stashes them beside it, and clambers in, stifling the sigh of pleasure the hot water elicits. Sinking down to where only his head is in view, he prepares to submerge himself if it comes to it. Shunkerr's voice comes through the door: "Malaas, are you in there?"

"Yes Uncle. What is it?"

"I've been looking for you. There is so much to show you here. I know you've gotten a bit distracted from our scribing lessons, what with Di'aahna showing you all sorts of herb lore and such, but the opportunities for scholarly pursuits in this city are manifold. They have a library here don't you know! The Ethu don't even keep written records under normal circumstances, all of their histories are orally passed down. But here, because they have integrated with humans—"

"Okay uncle, why don't you let me finish bathing and I'll accompany you. You can tell me all about it on the way to their library, sounds fascinating."

She rolls her eyes and continues to rinse.

"Alright," Shunkerr responds. "Meet me at the main entrance. I'll be waiting for you there."

All three grin as the footsteps tromp away from the door to the antechamber. They listen as Shunkerr exchanges a few words with the old woman before leaving the hall and can still hear her puttering around outside the door when he leaves. It's only a matter of time before she wishes to get washed up herself. Kithiik watches from the hot spring as Malaas finishes rinsing and then saunters over to him, her form every bit as enticing as that of Di'aahna's in its' own sumptuous way, voluptuous where Di'aahna's is athletic, tending toward rounded shapes and no edges. She has incredible breasts: large, fecund, with nipples a rich, deep brown against her already brown skin, ringed by small areola only slightly darker than the surrounding flesh. Age not yet allowed to truly have it's way with them, they hang as yet suspended, partially defying gravity, daring it to do it's worst, nipples ripe and pointedly announcing their presence, practically begging to be taken between someone's teeth.

Just as this thought prances through his mind, she leans down in front of him, dangling her delectables scant inches from his face. He looks up to see that delightedly wicked expression playing upon her face once more. Cupping those breasts in her hands, she looks down at Kithiik and smiles. Unruly dark brown curls tied back in her characteristic ponytail, random strands wet and plastered to the sides of her face, she leans in and speaks softly.

"I can't wait until you play with these. I want you inside me and I'm going to *have* you inside me. Soon. You want that? Good. Cuz I want you to want it. I think I want you to want it so bad you're ready to take it."

So saying she turns, and he uses the opportunity to admire the line of her back, leading to her incredible ass, rounded and jiggling the tiniest fraction every time her weight shifts and her foot hits the floor. Gracefully curving hips atop shapely legs with nicely thick thighs complete the picture and he cannot help giving several silent expressions of thanks to whatever deities are responsible for depositing him here. Drying off, both she and Di'aahna head for the door.

"You gonna get out of that tub or you gonna wait until you're wrinkled enough to be a living prune?" Di'aahna asks him, and they both grin as they walk out.

He exits shortly behind the two of them and immediately sees the widening of the old womans' eyes, the pursing of her lips in mild disapproval.

Di'aahna, seeing the same thing, simply laughs and finishes dressing. Not a whole lot of time remains before third crossing, but there is more than enough to have a decent conversation, so while Malaas goes off to meet Shunkerr, Kithiik goes with Di'aahna in search of a quiet place to talk for a while. So much has happened in such a short amount of time, Kithiik has been left with very little room to ponder any of it. Now that he's got the opportunity, a multitude of questions teem in his head, and

it's all he can do to keep from drowning in them. Opting to wander until Kithiik's meeting with Wheirdaahn, they talk as they walk. "Kithiik, I'm a sensitive. I'm a healer and I work in several different modalities. But the truth is, I've never done anything like what I was able to do with you during your fever. Manifesting like that in your dream world? It was amazing! I think it was only possible because you're a sensitive yourself.
Wheirdaahn's right about that, I'm sure of it."

"Okay," Kithiik answers, "But you don't even know what you did in there? In the fever dream, or whatever it was?"

"I'm not saying that. I know what I did. I'm just amazed I was able to do it like that. Maybe that's how it can happen when you work on another sensitive, I'm not even sure. The minute I tapped in, I was just suddenly there. It's never happened that way for me before. But once I was in, when I saw you wandering, well then I was on more familiar ground; one state, or plane removed I guess. After that, it became a matter of looking at the locks."

"Locks? What do you mean by locks?" Kithiik asks the question although he suspects he's already got an idea.

"You already know don't you? I can see locks of a great many different kinds, even outside of the energetic world. We deal in energies, all of us. Every interaction is governed entirely by energies. Some of us are simply taught to pay more attention to it than others. Like, when we were in your room: that spiritual, energetic space you somehow constructed in your delirium, I noticed several locks. There were those I chose not to mess with, and others I thought might potentially keep you in dangerous territory.

"You were close to being beyond my reach you know that? I've never seen the kind of poison running in your system, but I knew whatever it was, you couldn't be allowed to linger too much longer in that state without help. I didn't know how long you'd been down there, laid up against that wall, waiting to die. You're system is strong, good constitution, but the poison had sapped most of it from you. I don't think you had long left. I wasn't even sure I could do anything for you, until I saw the locks. You'd suppressed so much, taken on so much, it's like they were begging to be burst. I figured that one of two things would happen when I opened it. The first was that the resulting release would bring you out of the delirium, and closer to a place where herbs and healing could do the rest of the work."

"And the second?" he asks. "What was the second?"

"That you would die. But you would transition to the other side in peace, with no turmoil accompanying you on that final journey. I would have made your passing as easy as possible. But I was betting on the fact that you didn't want to die any more than I wanted to see you dead. Will has a lot to do with living.”

"But," Kithiik questions, "My mother, what about her? How did you do that? Thauma? Are you a thauma practitioner as part of your energy healing? You can't tell me that was just energetics. I saw her; touched her. Did you call her back from Beyond? What was that?"

"Your mother?" Di'aahna pauses, genuine surprise evident all over her face. "That would explain a lot then. You're much closer to the spirits than you may know, and blessed by them as well. She must have been so close! I am only a little familiar with the spirit realm, that's not where I'm at my best. I can see, but usually only faintly, just intimations. I get messages sometimes. But that? I actually didn't know what would happen when I unlocked that one. It was a lock within a lock, a room within a room, but it was emanating such powerful, radiant love, I knew it wasn't holding anything damaging, you know? So I guided you into it. I didn't even know it was your mother until now."

She pauses again before speaking: "What you received was a singular gift Kithiik, and even though I'm incredibly happy I got to aid in making it happen, I can only take credit for making you aware, giving you a kind of key, to unlock something already dwelling inside you. It was an honor to be a part of it. I could immediately feel so much healing in that space! It was almost unreal."

Both of them lapse into silence for a while following her last words, Kithiik lost in contemplation of his sojourn in the fever world, Di'aahna simply giving him space. He begins speaking to her without looking up. "I don't know how you did what you did. It was a gift I'll never be able to repay. Your key made it possible for me to speak to my mother, and my mother set me free—from myself. I'd never have been able to see that without you, never have been able to see her without you. I'm not the best with words, I got no practice." At last he looks up at her. "What I want to say is so much bigger than thank you, but that's all I've got right now."

"It's all you need."

And she smiles her kind smile, the welcoming smile that bestows warmth and comfort both.

"What you don't understand," she says, still smiling hugely, "is that this was like, it was the ultimate reaffirmation of what I was sent here to do! I don't know if I'll ever get to experience its' like again, and if not, I'll be content the rest of my days to have been through it just the once. That is how unique, how utterly holy shit what we did together was!

"Make no mistake, you were just as much responsible as I was. You enabled me to do what I did. I couldn't have accomplished it without your desiring it, regardless of whether you consciously knew what you were getting into or not. Without your permission, I doubt things would have played out as they did." "Well I'm glad of it, even though I had no clue. It happened like it happened, and now I get to live. I get to really live. I thought you were some kind of phantom healer lady or something, didn't even know if you were real. I'm glad you were there when you were." He ducks his head but manages to keep looking her in the eyes as he speaks. "I'm glad you're here now. You're the best damned healer I've ever met, that's for sure!"

Laughter can feel so good.

"Di'aahna, I know more questions are gonna pop up in my head as time goes on, is it alright if I ask you stuff when it shows up? Are you planning on disappearing anytime soon?"

"Of course you can! I'm not going anywhere for a while yet. You're not the only one who received a message up there," she continues, "I'll tell you more about that later. I know you need to meet with Wheirdaahn. Go spend some time with your foster father. There's no rush, and I'm happy to answer whatever questions you come up with. Maybe it'll help me to understand more about what happened as well."

They part ways just before the break in the path where he will meet Wheirdaahn. The minute they do, Kithiik is seized by dread of his impending meeting. The moment has been deferred several times but there is nothing for it now; he'll have to face his foster father. Before going after the Serpentari, he'd never lied to his foster father in his life. Now, he's preparing to lie his face off. There's no way Wheirdaahn can ever find out about what transpired in those Tunnels. And as long as Kithiik keeps his mouth shut over the truth, letting out just enough to make his story believable, he may be able to survive Wheirdaahn's dissatisfaction and potential fury. Taking as large a breath as his constricting lungs will allow, fighting through the tangled, tightening knot forming in his stomach, Kithiik makes his way toward the trail where he will meet his mentor; where things will be decided once and for all.

Chapter Five
ETHU

Kithiik contemplates as he walks, only vaguely registering the greenery on all sides of him, the beauty of his surroundings, the diffused light filtering through the forest canopy. He's come through so much, surviving the Serpentari and the murderous weight of his memories, and come out the other side really feeling alive for the first time. However, a single task remains before everything is complete. It would be a shame to be murdered by the only person alive he loves after all that. Of course Wheirdaahn won't kill him; he cares about him too much.

But if he casts him out? That would be worse than death, if Wheirdaahn were to disown him because of what he's done. Wheirdaahn would never in a thousand years be able to guess what really happened in the Tunnels, but Kithiik also defied his express wishes, lied to him about where he'd gone. If his foster father ends up asking for details, and he senses that Kithiik is holding something back from him, what will that do to his trust? Because no matter what, Kithiik will never risk telling him, telling anyone, the full extent of what happened.

He's been taught to loathe the Serpentari his entire life. There have been no exceptions. Except…except for the fact that there is still a mystery to unravel. When he entered the Serpentari's cavern, the first word out of her mouth had been "young", as if she'd been expecting someone older? She'd gone on to ask him if he'd come to serve. What did that mean? The obvious conclusion was that there were others who had come to serve. That opened up a yawning pit's worth of questions and suppositions, almost all of which led down extremely dark paths.

Should he tell Wheirdaahn that part? He knows there'd be no stopping his foster father if he thought people he knew and trusted were in league with the Serpentari. It might very well set him off, and then there would be bloodshed aplenty until he found the answers he was looking for, or ended up dead. His search could get him killed, if it ended up pitting him against the Serpentari.

Before Kithiik faced her, he would have thought Wheirdaahn stood a chance. But the ease with which she'd disarmed Kithiik, the inhuman strength he'd sensed in her grip, has given him a different perspective. While he broods, his feet carry him closer to his appointment and shortly he sees the object of his brooding waiting at the bottom of the path. Kithiik tries with all his might to keep the trepidation from his face, but the only technique he's got is to bring on the shield that shuts out everything. It's the mask he uses in combat and Wheirdaahn will recognize it in a heartbeat because he's the one who taught it to him. Realizing his quandary, Kithiik decides on different tack—he starts talking.

"This place is amazing! It's so different, and kinna crazy lookin' and strange." He's speaking slowly, meandering between sentences, babbling has never been his wont, as foreign to him as excessive happiness. "On the way down from the plateau, we got a view of the city for the first time in daylight. Gods, it was…I can't even—"

"Boy." Wheirdaahn's voice, quiet and gravelly, cuts Kithiik's diatribe short effortlessly. "Let's walk." Kithiik says nothing further, only falls into step beside Wheirdaahn as he heads deeper into the forest on a path Kithiik didn't even realize was there until he set foot onto it. Foreboding thick as molasses encloses him. His heart doubles its efforts in his chest, as if working with thicker blood of a sudden. The birds singing amongst the branches overhead take on an ominous cast, as does the muted illumination from the Light Serpents.

The forest that seemed such a welcoming place mere hours before now seems treacherous, full of places to disappear into, never to be seen again, never even to be missed. If it came down to it, perhaps he would just remain here, not worry about returning to Wah'Evi ever again. A forest like this could swallow a person up without ruffling the moss on a single branch of the gargantuan trees towering amidst their thinner neighbors, the roots burrowing so deep into the mountain, the very soil holds no knowledge of man save as nutrient for the worms.

Wheirdaahn stops and turns to him, places a callused hand on one of his shoulders, an incredibly grave expression molding his countenance into an unwontedly somber masque. This is it then. Kithiik takes a deep breath, braces himself for whatever is coming. He's been training with Wheirdaahn since he was four cycles old. He's grown up with the man, tried to be like him in many ways. He knows he sorely disappointed his teacher when he defied his wishes and attempted to kill the Serpentari in the Tunnels. He almost died because of it. But that's not all that happened down there. And the truth of what happened, much more even than allowing the Serpentari to disarm him in less time than it took to slip beneath the surface of an underground pool and fight his way to the surface again, lies like an unseen, massively heavy wedge between them.

"Look at me." Kithiik steels himself and looks his foster father full in the face for the first time since being pulled from the Tunnels what seems like cycles ago. For a moment, he cannot process the emotion baring itself in the eyes of his teacher. When it finally comes clear to him, immediately, wonderingly, all of his fear dissolves.

"When we came upon the body in the Tunnels and it turned out to be you—*my* boy, I was fit ta burst somebody's heart and tear it right outta their chests. I almost died in that instant, almost lost meself to grief." Kithiik is flabbergasted. The distance from petrified to mortified is infinitely shorter than he would have expected. He starts to apologize, to protest, anything to stop this from continuing. Wheirdaahn does not look like this. He never talks about grief; never allows the weathered terrain of his features to reveal such naked emotion. It almost feels like a transgression to see him this way, and worse yet, to be the cause of it.

"Wheir.." he begins, but Wheirdaahn will not be stopped.

"Ye went after the Serpentari didn't ye?" he asks him, waiting for the answer he already knows. "Yes." Kithiik looks down in shame and confusion. Wheir's not mad? He's somewhere around the opposite of angry apparently and nothing about this is what he thought it would be.

"Listen to me. There's no need for ye to say anythin' else. Yer young, and gods-awful fulla pride. You've been listenin' to the tales o' warriors and such since ye were a squaller and o'course ye went and set yer sights on the biggest flippin' game ye could think of. It went about as would be expected facing an opponent of that caliber. Ye done more than a great many before ye just by surviving. Never mind how ye lied to me, told me ye was gonna be holed up wi' some girl from outside the town and whatnot. Ye think I can't see how ye tense up when ya see me? How scared ye are to talk to me? I'm not gonna add to that. You've been punished enough by whatever happened down there. But hear me, and hear me good," Wheirdaahn grips him by both shoulders and looks him directly in his eyes. When he speaks again, his gravelly voice is slow, measured, and infinitely determined.

"Ye ever go after it again, I'm comin' after ye into them Tunnels. I'll follow ye, an if I die, my blood is on yer hands. Cuz you're the only reason in the world I'd willingly throw me life away. Understand what I mean when I say that. You know who I am. Ye know I mean what I say. Yer more important to me than pretty much anythin' else in this world." With that he snatches Kithiik into the fiercest hug he's ever endured. Kithiik grips him just as savagely, brought to the verge of tears for the second time in the span of a single week by an open admission of love. For a timeless time they stand that way, embracing on a forest path, in the middle of a mountain city, bound by love and pain and cycles and time.

Of all the moments of his short life, Kithiik will look back on this one over the succeeding cycles continuously, carrying it as a talisman resting in his chest beside that of his mother, cradling his head on her knees, whispering love through her palms.

When finally they pull apart, the forest feels alive again, rich with mystery and beauty and new, strange life. Wheirdaahn steps back from him a pace, looks him up and down.

"Looks like yer recovering quite nicely. I've a mind to show ye somewhat. Come with me." They resume walking and presently, Kithiik begins to notice strange, scintillating light casting even stranger shadows on the forest floor, along the trunks of trees, and permeating the leaves wherever light leaks through the canopy overhead. He realizes they must've come beneath the shallows of the floating lake.

They continue on the trail, heading deeper into the forest until coming to a place where the forest thins out and clears completely. Directly in front of them stands the tallest tower Kithiik has ever seen. This is one of the towers he'd seen from the trail earlier! Constructed in a way thoroughly alien to him, the tower seems more grown than built, twisting as it does like some gigantically tall tree topped with weird, bulbous chambers.

"Wheir…what are those things at the top? What's this tower here for?"

"Ye can aready see the floating lake o'course. What ye probably don't know is that every spring, the lake starts to sinking, a little at a time and by the end o' summer, it sinks mebbe a hundred feet downwards. Its waters come down so low, they submerge the tops o' these towers here. There's a race o' merfolk who live in the waters o' the lake, and when the waters sink, those as wish it can climb up into the tower chambers and look at the creatures up close and personal. Aside from that, there's another race o' winged merfolk that're attracted to these towers. It gives them a place to bask in open air, as opposed to having to fly around the underside o' the waters all the time.

"Thing is, ye get to a certain height in specific places, and the gravity changes on ye. As a for instance, ye ever take it upon yourself to travel to the top o' one of these towers, you'll notice somethin' funny happens 'bout three quarters o' the way up. You'll start floating same as the waters o' the lake. You'll have to pull yourself down outta the tower before our gravity takes hold again. Ask the uncle o' Malaas 'bout the specifics, he's the scholar, not me. I just know what I know."

Kithiik looks incredulously from his foster father to the tower and back again.

"Merfolk? Winged merfolk? Are you having a laugh? I mean, come on, seventeen summers and I've never heard of anything of the kind, not even in the jongleurs' tales or the chroniclers' legends. I don't get it." Wheirdaahns' face takes on an ironically cynical expression.

"Ahh, it is a laugh, itn't it? Here ye are, just back from an encounter wi' a creature half the Provinces don't believe in, middle of a city populated by a bunch of hybrid humans, and yer having the hardest time believing in something as simple as merfolk? If I had half a drink in me, I'd laugh ye right outta this city, I would. It's truth alright, real as these towers standing here. Ye probably even thought the plants on yer guide's cloak was sewn on didn't ye? Ha! Do yourself a favor, boy, don't ever limit what you'll believe based on what you've seen for yourself. Keep an

open eye, don't mistake me, but keep it open in both directions, ye hear me?

"Haa, yer a funny one. Let's go, we best be getting back. It'll be time for the festivities soon, and your no gonna wanna miss those. We can yap as we walk. These are the kinds of things most town and city folk never hear about, and if they do, they don't believe. It's too far-fetched for their minds. Only reason I know is cuz I've done my share o' caravan jobs fer House Wah'Evi, and I've done my share o' drinkin' with the guards up here, and some o' the working folk besides. They get to telling tales and stories just like down the mountain, only difference is, a buncha their stories are chock full o' things so fantastic you'd swear they was lying through every tooth in their mouths—'cept they aren't. This place breeds wonders for fun; folk round here don't even have to make anything up, they're every day is crazier n' most jongleurs legends."

The two of them walk in companionable silence for a moment before Kithiik remembers something. "Wheir, when I was fevered and all that, and Di'aahna came for me, something happened, something incredible." They both stop walking as Wheirdaahn reacts to the earnestness in his foster son's tone.

"I…I got to see my ma. I did." Wheirdaahn goes absolutely, ominously still, his expression a frozen mask, but Kithiik plows on, desperate to get it all out. "She didn't need to tell me who she was, I just knew; she was wearing all white, and her skin was so dark, so very dark, like none I've ever seen but mine. The healer she…she opened a door, a door inside me and she was there, Shayla was, and I went to her." He's babbling, he knows that, and he's crying again, he knows that too, but he's got to get this out. He's not the only one with locks; fever isn't the only kind of key.

"I laid my head on her knees, I did, and she put her hands on my head. She comforted me and told me…she told me she was proud of me already. Told me she wanted me to move on, to let it go. I'd been holding on to it for so long, thought it was my fault that she died, my life wasn't worth the cost of hers. I just want to say I'm sorry. You've tried to raise me the best you could all these cycles, and I kept trying to die, kept putting myself at risk over and over so I could prove I was worthy; that my life had some kind of meaning. Every time I got in that arena for a Death Duel, every time you wouldn't come watch me for those, I knew it then but it's so different now. You never have to worry about me fighting in one of those again. You never have to worry about me going after legends. I'm sorry, so sorry for putting you through all that."

And for the second time that day, he finds himself clinging fiercely to the man who's raised him from an infant, trained him from a child, and claims him as a son. As Kithiik was speaking, laying bare cycles' worth of regret and folly, he watched the rigidity melt from his foster father's frame and he fervently hopes his words reached some of the sore spaces within Wheirdaahn that need their own letting go of, their own lock picks.

After another prolonged embrace, Wheirdaahn speaks, relieving the remainder of the tension as he does so: "By the gods, boy, wha's happnin to us? We'll bawl ourselves a new lake at this rate." This pulls a smile from Kithiik and they walk as they talk.

"It's been a long time. I've wondered if there was anything I could do to help. I'd done all I knew how. I saw the hunger in ye, but I had no idea what to do about it, 'cept train you so well you'd override your own death wish by winning all the time. Mebbe if you won enough, someday you'd actually reach yer goal of being in the songs, and having tales written about ye. But it feels so much better to know yer actually willing to live now. Balls, ye gave yer old man a scare and a half getting there, didn'tcha?" He pauses in his step once more and turns to Kithiik. "Ye really saw her?"

"I did, plain as you're standing there now. Plain as that tower we just left, I saw her."

Wheirdaahn starts walking again, shaking his head as he goes. "Wow. That Di'aahna's a healer an a half, itn't she? Sure as sure she is. I've never met one so strong in it. It's her callin', that's clear. She's also the biggest damned flirt; ye know I seen her messin' with some of the more stick in the mud pilgrims fer the fun of it I swear. Ye done picked yourself an interesting healer in that one, I tell ye. I managed to get ye a change o' clothes by the way. They'll be waitin fer ye when ye get back to the barracks. You're lucky one o' the Wah'Evi boys is close to your size. He doesn't have your shoulders, but his leggings should fit just fine. You'll probably hafta work some on the way down, to pay off your upkeep whilst you was off yer feet. Nothin' major, mind, just enough to satisfy the boss man, make sure he don't take it entirely outta my pay."

"Gladly," Kithiik answers, "you just point me in the right direction and tell me what to do, I'm there." The light of final crossing is beginning to fade, dusk making its presence known by slow degrees as the two of them come out from under the trees, onto the branching of the main paths.

"Get to the barracks, see if either o' your girls are there, change into a fresh set o' clothes and head up to the main hold. It'll be easy to find, just follow the lights and the music. Oh, and the old man, Shunkerr, may try ta offer ye an armband or some such thing. Do yourself a favor and don't take it. Trust me on that one. If ye can manage it, make sure yer Malaas does the same. I'll say no more. Be off with ye." Wheirdaahn cuffs him on the back of the head and sends him off.

Mind ablaze with the anticipation of upcoming events, Kithiik gets to the barracks and finds the waiting package on his cot in record time. After changing into a new set of clean leggings, and a tight-fitting vest that he actually doesn't mind as much as he thought he would, he heads out immediately, nodding to the few straggling pilgrims still making ready. Following the main path is easy. Everywhere lights abound, cleverly carved, intricately tooled little lanterns illuminate all the paths and the music of flutes, fiddles, drums and other instruments run in circles round his ears. Faint at first, the music gradually increases in volume the closer he gets to the main hall.

Hundreds of people, all heading in the same direction, stream along the paths babbling excitedly in what seems like a thousand conversations. The crowd is, of course, like no crowd he has ever witnessed. Varying degrees of voluptuousness and pale skin tones present themselves for inspection. From what he's heard, the Ethu are naturally tall, slender, and absent of pigment as albinos minus the pink eyes, but decades worth of interbreeding between the Ethu and the humans of the kingdom have created hybrids aplenty.

The apparel ranges from gaily colored, festive raiment he'd expect to see at any fete during festival season in town, to entirely different, utterly alien (to his eye) fashions. Draped, brightly colored hides with peculiar natural patterns accentuated by strategically placed, painted patches of color; handsome beaded jewelry of bone, wood, woven plants and linked shards of polished stones; long, ornamented loincloths of feathered, beaded, and otherwise worked fabrics so treated that it's hard for Kithiik to tell whether they come from plant or animal; armfuls of bangles and twining vines made into winding bracelets travel up the arms of exceptionally beautiful albino women with tapered ears, slanted eyes, and luscious, painted lips all colored in vivid, vibrant hues.

The colors stand out against the stark white of their skins, making of them delightfully foreign, exotic creatures. As if they need be any more exotic and alien than they already appear. More than three quarters of the revealing fashions on display here would be severely frowned upon if not outright banned in Wah'Ehvi Towne, and the Provinces of a surety. Only the harlots would dare such a thing, and then only within the confines of their brothels. Not so here where the predominant theme appears to be accentuation of the lithe, willowy forms. Male and female alike treat modesty like a foreign concept.

A great many of them remind him of his mother's strong features, only alabaster skinned with slanted eyes. They even have similarly textured hair; thick and wooly like his when he lets it grow. But theirs is completely white, unless dyed otherwise, with the hairlines beginning far back on their foreheads, many of them twisted into some of the thickest dreadlocks he's ever seen. Tied and teased into dozens of styles, the locks form sculptures upon their heads, or hang down in thick, dangling ropes to their waists, some even longer, with more than a few reaching ankle length.

His attention is continually drawn by an almost subliminal jingling barely audible beneath the hubbub of speech and laughter, until he notices yet another detail. A large number of the Ethu have all manner of miniature bells, chimes, rattles and other noisemakers woven, braided, and otherwise affixed to their hair. Once alerted, he realizes they're everywhere to be seen, on anklets, and bracelets as well, the majority cunningly worked so as to be virtually unnoticeable.

The pronounced cheekbones, strong features, white hair with cut back hairlines and woven, jingling decorations, juxtaposed with their curiously tapered ears, the piercings and tattoos everywhere in evidence, and the subtle, but unmistakable grace of their movements, make for one of the single most stunning congregations of beings Kithiik believes he will ever see. Eyes swimming with alien beauty, senses enlivened by the strains of foreign music filling the air, Kithiik allows himself to be swept along with the living tide toward the grand gathering hall.

Again, the architecture of the Ethu Maahg outstrips his ability to describe or contain within any of the boundaries of his prior experience. Not that he's been to many grand halls in his lifetime, but he gets the impression most of the ones crafted entirely by man would at least have full ceilings. The hall is magnificently wrought, as if the darling child of an unheralded union between deranged engineers and a coterie of singularly ambitious gardeners. It occurs to Kithiik that he must only have caught the merest fraction of the actual city from his vantage on the path leading down from the plateau. So much of the construction is in fact hidden from casual view if one knows not what to look for. The outer walls and visible towers are but window dressing for the real majesty of the treetop chambers and winding, hanging, tricksy pathways making incredible, interconnected edifices of separate trees within a forest turned sumptuous city.

Knowing he is gawking, but hard pressed to stop, he brings his gaze back to the revelers and is immediately intrigued by a most unusual sight. Several meters ahead, a large, hunchbacked man with arms that seem abnormally long and a face accustomed to scowling is half led, half dragged to the hall by a squealing mess of children. They pull on his arms and hands, hang about his shoulders, tug on his legs and one, wrapped around his calf, rides upon his foot, giggling hysterically with every step he takes. The man, light brown skinned, heavily muscled and hard looking, appears completely at his ease amidst the screaming mini-cacophony, indulgently allowing the children to plait his hair and pull on his clothing, all the while making his slow, somehow stately way to one of the many entrances of the hall. Kithiik is unaccountably taken aback by the tableau, and so is completely unprepared for what happens to him next.

An Ethu girl of indeterminate age, scantily clad in laced vines that reveal as much as they cover, steps in front of him. Bedecked with bangles of wood and jade, thick white locks beginning far back on her forehead done up in a half mohawk along one side of her head and left to hang down the other shoulder, a single slender wooden lip ring going through the middle of her bottom lip, steps in front of him, the girl blocks his path. She looks as struck by him as he was by the sight of the hunchback.

Wondering, almost unbelieving, she reaches out, running a delicately tapered, slender finger up his arm to his face, caresses his cheek.

The thousand conversations, the music surrounding them, become a distant happening, an irrelevant accompaniment. Bewitching and

exquisite as the city she calls home, marveling at the reality of his
darkness in the greater darkness of this night, she cradles his cheek, brings
her face close and breathes his breath. A shiver runs through him. When

she kisses him, it is a soft thing, a tentative question--an invitation. She pulls back and a smile blossoms at the ends of her lips and widens to encompass the whole of her mouth as an answering smile spreads across his face.

"Are you here alone?" she asks through her smile, her voice husky, the slightest rasp lending it a sexy roughness he wants to hear more of. "No…no I'm not." She kisses him again and the people, the conversations, the drums, the jingling and piping all crash back in upon them as she molds her body to his and sucks on his lower lip like a lost lover.

"Do I get to meet her?" she asks after pulling her lips away for a second time, body mercilessly pressing into his, delectably insistent; there is no air between them. "Would you like to?" he asks her. The crowd parts and flows round them as if used to navigating the whims of living currents, and the flotsam caught by the waves. He feels a hand lightly brush his shoulder in passing, and then another, and he looks up to find that some of the Ethu in the seemingly never-ending stream are letting their hands brush the two of them for the briefest of moments as they pass, trailing fingertips as if giving a blessing. Perhaps they take a little bit of the deliciousness with them, like sticking one's finger in a sweet batter just before baking. For the briefest of moments he also notices that the same cannot be said for some of the full humans walking past—most of these studiously avoid looking at him, ignoring the occurrence as best they can manage. Releasing his worries of unknowingly transgressing the customs of the city, he re-immerses himself in her scent: earth, forest and leaf, nectar and sex—the smell of secret things. She tastes intoxicatingly of ripe berries with the sweetest undercurrent of a fermented something. The nipples of her small breasts are hard through the fabric of his vest.

He wonders if she is Malaas' type, wonders if Malaas has a type. Recognizes that it would never even have occurred to him to wonder about such things before seeing Malaas with Di'aahna earlier this same day. Looking at the lunatic turn for the better his life has taken, he again makes a mental note to ask Di'aahna for the names of her gods; he has no doubt his fortune in this arena is not due to the Gods of Blade. Continuing to kiss him, letting her mouth meander across the outsides of his lips, the Ethu girl confounds his tongue. He has only tentatively begun to wander with his hands when she places hers over his own.

"Yes, I would…" Deliberately moving his hands beneath hers, she pushes them to roam the expanse of her body, running his palms over the smoothness of the flesh of her back beneath the festooned vines of her garment, the soft skin of her buttocks. Pulling back just enough so that she can look into his face, she takes one of his hands and continues down the curve of her ass, guiding the tips of his fingers toward the cleft between her legs from behind. He is shocked at the wetness he finds waiting there, running down her inner thighs.

She grins at his expression and begins grinding herself into his crotch, staring up at him, her face changing. Gripping him by the hips, she undulates against the bulge of his cock through his leggings, biting her lip as the pleasure travels her body in waves. He pulls her to him tighter, taking a firmer grip of her ass and sliding two fingers into the clenched wetness of her cunt, savoring the expelled breath and the half closing of her eyes that follows. She seems almost drunk with the pleasure of his hand and the grinding of her clit against the bulge of his cock, straining at the fabric of his leggings like a starving animal. Her pussy is hot, an incredibly wet furnace pulsating round his fingers. He pushes them deeper into her. She moans and squirms in his grip, eyes going wide, mouth open in a silent inhale.

"Oh fuck yes…" Her nails dig into his sides and she buries her face in the crook of his neck, moaning and biting hard into his shoulder as he fucks her with his fingers. He doesn't speed up, opting instead to revel in the feel of his fingers in her flesh, sliding them repeatedly deep into the slickness of her cunt over and over in a slow, pounding rhythm he imagines is the way he'd like to fuck her; his fingers the surrogate for his cock if it were loose. The feel of her teeth in his shoulder is like a spur he ignores in favor of holding himself to the pace he dictates. Nevertheless, he feels the ripples around his knuckles intensifying, is sure that she must be leaving bite marks on his shoulders and scratch marks all over the sides of his back as she grips him tighter and surrenders to her own orgasm.

Her climax when it comes pulses with the same beat of his fingers: slow, pounding, insistent. Her body shudders in time to the rhythm they've just created, pleasure washing her in almost palpable waves, her breath hot against his neck, the satisfied sighing of her husky voice the signal to the ending of their personal song. When the juddering of her body in his arms has dwindled to a few random spasms, he slips his fingers out of her, letting her take her own weight again. Clasping his hand in both of her own, she brings his fingers to her lips and sucks them dry of her juices one by one. Slowly. When she is finished, she kisses him once more. He can taste her pussy on her lips and tongue. She smiles a beatific smile.

"See you inside."

Turning, she manages to lose herself amongst the thinning stream of revelers in seconds. Kithiik stares at the space she just vacated for a long moment, shaking his head to clear it. That could never have happened in the Provinces, save maybe in the Quants, or possibly in a town like Brothel Haven and even then, he suspects he'd have had to pay for the privilege. MaahgTain apparently specializes in fantasy, and Kithiik has never been more glad to be anywhere in his life.

Didn't even get her name, and he shakes his head again. He allows himself several minutes to recover equilibrium before passing through one of the entrances into the main hall a short while later. Of course, he walks head on into yet another view that stops him full in his tracks.

The grand hall is a wonder of Ethu/human engineering full of tables and candles, benches and chairs, platter upon platter of food, and throngs and throngs of people. The music spills loud and gay, musicians positioned on all manner of perches and platforms cunningly placed throughout the multi-leveled hall. Tables arranged on tiers situated all over the half-grown, half-built space, together with small bridges and stairs intricately connected to the huge sheltering foliage of the thickest trees, combine to form the skeleton of a massive, multi-domed hall; contriving to create enclosed spaces in an almost completely open theater. Amazing.

It takes him a few passes before he locates Shunkerr on a bench at a long table not far from the middle of the hall, heaped plate in front of him, Malaas to one side. He appears to be engaged in what looks like earnest conversation with several others, one of whom is the very same hunchback Kithiik saw earlier, seated on the other side of Shunkerr. The children hangers-on are no longer in evidence, but upon further appraisal, Kithiik espies several tables set aside for them against the walls, their playful squealing lost in the general hubbub of the room.

In another section of the hall, he can see the tables reserved for the guards, and it takes him but a second to find Wheirdaahn. His ever-watchful foster father having spotted him first, raises his mug in silent salute with a smile, and in an all-encompassing gesture, bids Kithiik enjoy himself. Deciding to do just that, Kithiik heads for one of the many banquet tables laden with food before making his way through the press to where Shunkerr and Malaas are seated.

The food tables brim over with victuals made up of more vegetable fare than Kithiik is used to seeing. He'd never have imagined the forest could provide such a bevy of different foods. Herbs mixed with roots, tubers, and other equally strange vegetables he's completely unfamiliar with overflow the tables in a plethora of simple dishes. At variable intervals between the vegetable dishes are meat dishes he's more accustomed to, alongside several that are thoroughly alien to him. One such dish is a huge, succulent looking platter of fish steaks. Whatever fish they came from must have been massive. The individual steaks could half fill a single platter without trouble.

No attendant serves the food. Guests are left to their own devices with stacks of plates shaped like broad leaves alongside wooden utensils situated at the corner of every table. Kithiik proceeds to heap his plate with anything he fancies. He's in the middle of cutting through one of the fish steaks, marveling at how easily the wooden knife parts the flesh, when Malaas comes up beside him. Smiling, he turns to her and his hands stop what they're doing of their own accord.

The hair she usually keeps back and up in her customary unruly ponytail is now completely unbound. The raucous curls form a curly mane round her head, falling to just beneath her shoulders, only a single band of worked wood keeping them from her face. A simple choker of silver encircles her neck, several inches of fine chain left to dangle at her collarbone. She wears a low cut, full length dress done in a beautifully graduating series of greens, and woven of an extremely soft, yielding fabric falling from the spaghetti-thin straps at her shoulders all the way to her ankles, barely draping the toes of short, open-backed boots.

Her delectable bosom stretches the fabric far out in front,

the nipples forming not so subtle peaks to either side of her chest. A slit, originating somewhere high up on her left hip, bisects the side of the garment, giving more than ample view of one of her lusciously shapely legs every time she shifts her weight in the right direction. She does so now, giving him a slow turn to take it all in, apparently using the much looser fashion customs of MaahgTain to delicious effect.

"Hello, Kithiik." His mouth is dry again. How does that happen so fast? She takes a step toward him, close enough to graze his arm with a breast. His hands suddenly remember they hold a laden plate.

"Do you like it? I hope you do." She steps even closer, lips brushing his ear; the danger of dropping the plate and making a mess of things increasing tenfold.

"I was thinking of you when I picked it out, when I tried it on." She takes a small nip at his earlobe, "I'm hoping I get a chance to try *you* on tonight." Lightly grabbing the back of his head, she pulls his mouth down to hers for a short kiss, tastes his lips, the unfamiliar flavors resting there. She pulls back with a mischievous question on her face. "Mmm, you taste good. What have you been getting into tonight?"

Uncertainty snaps him from contemplation of bringing that particular fantasy to fruition. Unsure exactly how to proceed, he turns back to the table and busies himself with continuing to heap food on his suddenly captivating plate. Malaas, contenting herself with filling two goblets, seems completely unfazed. "What was I tasting?" she ponders aloud, stepping close to him again, speaking in low tones despite the din. "Part of it was sweet, like the berry wine they've been serving all night, but there was another taste too, something a little more tangy. Wait, was that her pussy I was tasting?" She immediately begins almost choking with laughter at the resulting expression on Kithiik's face. He comes this close to dropping the plate after all at the casual way she's broached the subject. The other side of the coin is that apparently the gods have decided to bless him with an exceptionally brilliant fantasy of a life; all that remains is for him to live it. With that thought in mind, he sets the wheels in motion, feeling perpetually out of his depth but nevertheless resolving to plow ahead anyway. There's nothing for it but to practice. He's had so little practice at any of this.

"Actually, she wants to meet you," he says to Malaas, when he finally collects his wits and they begin the walk back to the table where Shunkerr is still thoroughly engrossed in his conversation.

"Really?"

"Yeah. She asked me if I was here alone, and I told her no."

This earns him an interesting look. "So she asked if she could meet you." Taking a breath, feeling thoroughly novice, he plunges on. "Do you have a type? Of girl, I mean." There, he said it. Who would ever have thought a conversation like this would be possible, let alone happening to him? Now it is Malaas who pauses, though only briefly.

"I have no idea. All I know is that what happened earlier felt really…good. I liked it. I think I want more of it, and I know I want more of you. You seem to have good taste so far, so keep it up and I imagine we'll be fine."

Chapter Six
CLAAHNS'DANE

Claahns'Dane: roughly translated as "The Violent Dance" in the common tongue, is a phenomenon exclusive to the Ethu Peoples of the Upper and Lower TlammaTain mountain range and little-known outside of scholarly circles.
-From the journal of Duhmane the Itenerant Scholar

K ithiik is conscious of the festivities going on all around them, the conversation between him and Malaas but one of hundreds caroming off each other within the grand hall of MaahgTain and flying out into the benighted forest beyond the festival lights. Wonderment shades his voice as they make their way through the colorful press. "Where did you come from? What happened to shy little Malaas?"

She returns his look, and for the first time in a while, he's gets a glimpse of the slightly shy but competent girl he used to see arranging the tallies and setting the matches at the Fights.

"I'm still shy, just not around you anymore. I've been inside your fever dream. I got to touch a boy I've wanted to touch since the first time I saw him, say things I've dreamed of speaking aloud for cycles. See how you look at me now? I've always wanted you to look at me that way. Always. What if we hadn't found you when we did? I don't understand the gods and their whims, but I do know that sometimes, crazy things happen for weird reasons. If we'd never found you, or if Di'aahna hadn't been with us, things would be so different right now. I am so glad you're alive, but it's not just that, your experience changed all three of us.

"Di'aahna got a really powerful affirmation of her calling, you got your life back, and I got to see what it feels like to…be bold. I like the way it feels, some of the things I can do when I'm standing in the middle of it. It's like a kind of thauma or something, like mahj'ick all its own. Only I don't have to be trained in some weird arts, or sacrifice to some deranged god. I get to just sort of say what I want, and watch what happens."

By this point, they've almost reached the table, and Kithiik is amazed to see that Shunkerr remains thoroughly absorbed in his conversation with the hunchback. He wonders what manner of scholar the hunchbacked man must be to engross Shunkerr so completely. Malaas dangles a tantalizing piece of information before taking her seat. "You see how my uncle loves to talk? He also relishes the feeling of being able to teach. I asked all kinds of questions about the Ethu and got some interesting answers. For example, uncle thinks the girls here are too loose with their sexuality, given too much freedom by the unsurpassed herb lore of the Ethu. Who need worry about getting with child when herb mixtures are readily available that render pregnancy a controllable thing?" She looks pointedly at him before going to take her seat on the other side of the bench.

Shaking his head, Kithiik chooses a seat directly across from her. Inadvertently, this also gives him the chance to observe Malaas's newly embraced sexual power in action on someone other than himself. Though he always got the impression she was competent, he can remember nothing close to the level of burgeoning confidence and sensuality she exudes now. More than a few heads at the table turn in mid- sentence to watch her passage, and some at other tables as well.

The hunchback is one who takes notice among many others, and his shift in attentiveness rouses Shunkerr to goings-on outside the sphere of their conversation. He favors Malaas with a fond smile only slightly marred by his appraisal of her revealing dress before turning his attention to Kithiik.

"Ah, he rises and walks among us again. So glad you could join us. I was beginning to wonder if we'd have the pleasure of your company before the festivities ended. Have you had an opportunity to explore the city at all?" From the moment Shunkerr turns his attention onto him, Kithiik feels himself slamming internal walls into place. Such a chunk of time has passed, so many momentous things have occurred since the scholar's pointed remarks of days ago that the memory, while not faded, has definitely not been foremost in his mind. But now, Kithiik takes stock of the way Shunkerr regards him, again reminded of their conversation and the unfinished business left implied.

The scholar alone of all those present seems to have guessed something close to the truth of Kithiik's experience in the Tunnels. Now that everything with Wheirdaahn has been handled, Shunkerr represents the only reason things could go horribly wrong. Kithiik wonders about the old man's agenda for the first time in what seems like days, and determines to find out if only to dismiss the looming feeling of threat his imagination keeps conjuring.

Before he can answer the old man however, Di'aahna appears from amidst the throng, bearing a plate full of food, and claims a seat to the left of Kithiik. She arrives garbed in an ensemble that leaves so little to the imagination she momentarily halts all conversation. Her sleeveless top is a strappy thing that looks like someone stitched several strips of fabric together and decided to call it a piece of clothing. It covers little more than half the delectable mounds of her breasts, leaving everything from the nipples down exposed. The lower half of the outfit does only slightly more to cover the rest of her. An elaborately tooled, stiff leather corset designed rather like an exceptionally wide belt begins low on her back and extends down over her buttocks stopping just shy of covering her cheeks entirely.

The sides ride the curves of her hips, stopping several inches short of enclosing her entire waist. Two narrow straps bridge the remaining distance, leaving a delicious window of tanned flesh between the bottom-most strap and the paltry, triangular patch of fabric serving as the only cover for her nether lips. Every ounce of her toned, athletic form is on spectacular display, and it makes for a stunning picture indeed. Kithiik doesn't even know what the punishment would be for a woman showing up like this outside of a brothel in the Provinces, and finds himself almost awed by the defiant indifference she demonstrates through the deceptively simple channel of clothing. She greets him with a kiss on the cheek, and aims a dazzling smile at Malaas before turning to the rest of the table.

"Hope I'm not interrupting," she says, and immediately begins tucking into her food, "I've been having the most fascinating conversations with healers of several different modalities, from all over these mountains. I had no idea so many different clans converged on this city during the Renewal! Umgh! And the food is so good here too!" She continues speaking into the space her entrance has created, stuffing her mouth as if oblivious of the stares and completely unmindful of her scandalous attire.

"Don't mind me, please do continue with your conversation. Oh. This is so good." She looks at Kithiik. "Have you tried the fish? It's a species called ray you can only find in the floating lake. One of the clans brought some as a gift for the banquet. The major holidays are pretty much the only time the people here get to eat any of it, so it's considered a delicacy. It's really good, and the body of the ray has all sorts of medicinal effects too. Almost makes me want to change modalities."

"Ah," Shunkerr interjects, clearing his throat and trying his best to collect himself, "where are my manners?" Kithiik notices the scholar always seems particularly discomfited by the healer, as if he doesn't quite know what to do with her, although in this case, Kithiik can't blame the man one wit. Turning to the hunchback, Shunkerr proceeds to make introductions.

"Duhmane, may I please introduce my niece, Malaas, who I am thoroughly pleased to find has taken an interest in scribing, and her friend Di'aahna, a healer of quite some skill apparently. And this quiet young man here is Kithiik; all have come to MaahgTain as pilgrims this time round."

The hunchback, exhibiting surprising grace, kisses each of the girls' fingers in turn before extending one of his extraordinarily long arms across the table and swallowing Kithiik's hand in a palm that feels large enough to encompass an entire tankard with room to spare. His voice is a quiet rumble coming from the middle of his chest.

"I am Duhmane, traveler and unlikely scholar; I am more than pleased to make your acquaintance, as well as that of the ravishingly beautiful company you keep." Both Malaas and Di'aahna accept his compliment in smiling silence, bowing their heads slightly in acknowledgment. Di'aahna pauses for the barest instant before returning to tucking away her food as if it's going somewhere.

"You have chosen a fine time for your first visit." Duhmane continues, his quiet tone and demeanor at odds with the perpetual fierceness of his visage. A scowl remains permanently etched into the dense expanse of his overhanging brow. When combined with the bushy eyebrows and deep-set, intelligent eyes, his countenance makes for a marked counterpoint to the measured, almost genteel mannerisms he exudes.

"You are in for a singular experience this night, and soon, if my timing is correct. Shunkerr and I have been deeply engrossed in discussions of some of the customs and rituals enacted here.

Over many cycles of study my time here has allowed me to acquire quite the store of knowledge regarding these people and the founding of this most unique mountain city kingdom, and it makes for wonderfully stimulating conversation. But now," and here he looks directly at Kithiik, "you may want to follow the example of your friend and get some of that delicious food into you before you miss your chance."

Even as he utters the words, Kithiik begins to notice a general shushing spreading the length of the hall. People quiet their conversations, turn to look for the source of the suddenly imposed silence. Those unfamiliar with the ritual are hushed by the abrupt cessation in speech, truncated conversations acting as a far better indicator than any spoken directive. Bells begin to softly chime in the burgeoning silence, first one, then several, and quite without warning, Kithiik comprehends the purpose of all the jingling pieces of jewelry he thought only decorative adorning the dreadlocks of so many Ethu. The bells, emanating from no single source in the enormity of the open hall, seem to come from everywhere, the softest tinkling followed by the faintest rattling, a growing tintinnabulation.

Kithiik looks carefully around, recognizing yet another moment he needs to record in his memory banks for future perusal. Several individual Ethu reward his vigilance when he witnesses the moment they gently ping one piece of jewelry against another. More rattling enters the montage of sound and he marks it as several other Ethu vigorously shake their heads at differing intervals, setting their locks ringing and adding to the growing body of a tinkling composition in the making. Indeed, the jingle, rattle, chime take on a pattern, coalescing into a rhythm. It is a subtle thing, the insidious way in which the disparate sounds conspire to form a single utterance. A structured, almost orchestral song slowly emerges from the burgeoning chaos of ringing bells and struck chimes, its beauty in the myriad parts that form its substance, cadences building and subsiding, rolling like the fields of wheat when they sway to the winds' rhythms.

Kithiik fancies he can hear cycles of tradition contained within the tones, histories ancient beyond telling, see the uncanny grace of the Ethu in the way the patterns change; knell, strike, tinkle, shake, rattle— stop. With almost disconcerting abruptness, all sound suddenly ceases.

A single jingling, rattling, stomping cadence erupts into the profundity of that silence. Unlike the sounds of before that seemed to come from everywhere at once, this emanates from a specific location far back of the grand hall; from the same entrance Kithiik actually used if his hearing informs him aright. The cacophony draws swiftly nearer and in no time, it too has metamorphosed into a rhythm of its own; this one, a much more strident, aggressive thing, grounded in the driving realm of percussion, shifting the energy of the hall in seconds. Heads turn, the massed host pivots almost as one to greet the oncoming spectacle.

An elaborately garbed Ethu explodes into the expectant space, face inscribed with raised patterns pricked into his white flesh, eyes and mouth streaked with broad bands of bright green and red. Strapped to tight-fitting sleeves on both arms and woven into the thickness of his locks are myriad bells, rattles, tinkling bits of stone, metal and wood. A long, open, sleeveless robe with flapping hems and a plethora of weighted scarves drops from his shoulders to the floor, absolutely bestrewn with a ringing multitude of rattles, bells, chimes, and hanging strikers of metal, wood, stone, bone, plant, and even glass. A collar of more dangling bits of jangling pieces hangs from his neck, and beautifully wrought, miniature versions of the sound makers everywhere in evidence upon his costume pierce and hang from his ears, from tapered peaks to stretched earlobes. All manner of

sounding devices are likewise woven into the fabric of his
loincloth and resonating anklets sit above his bare feet such that

every movement he makes is marked by sound.

He leaps and gesticulates in an abandon of wildly extravagant movements: clapping, flipping, and stomping, every motion underscored by the uncanny grace and almost eerie economy of movement that characterizes the Ethu. Even in abandon, his limbs seem imbued with a sense of serenity completely at odds with the apparent fierceness of his gestures. Acrobatically somersaulting through the waiting throng, he creates a tumult of sound by himself, but incredibly, rhythm abounds within it, pattern and method. Every beat falls in time, every step and rattling twist minutely calculated. Further, as he makes his thoroughly circuitous way forward, jangling and jingling and tinkling as he comes, he also interacts with a great many of his kindred in his passing. The seemingly random outfling of his hand makes sudden and rapid connection with a chime woven into an Ethu's sharply swung braid; the slap of an upthrust open palm blends in complete time with the percussive rhythm of his passage. He uses his hands as strikers, punctuating his rhythm with the stomped jingle of his anklets, the slapping of his palms and ringed fingers to his chest, upper and lower arms creating counterpoint to their chiming. With a final leap, he turns an amazing somersault with a tumbler's grace, arms outstretched, the entire length of his long form barely arcing in the air, outflung arms the mirror for his hair.

The minute his feet touch ground he performs an incredibly tight spin, sending the hems of his robe flying outward round him before dropping to one knee, the rattling jingle of his movement a signal for the spellbound audience. What sounds like a thousand rattles and shakers go off at once in an ecstatic, controlled cacophony of sound.

The bedlam lasts until the figure at the center of the space rises. When he raises his head to the roof of the single actual dome in the otherwise open hall, all the Ethu raise their heads with him, giving voice to an unearthly, ululating cry of jubilant celebration.

"Wow!" Di'aahna whispers the thought aloud for Kithiik, and he only then remembers to shove something into his mouth before events render him incapable of consuming food. He casts a quick glance across the table and witnesses Shunkerr in a rare moment, completely enthralled and utterly taken by the spectacle.

"I bring welcome and salutations to the peoples gathered here this night!" the speaker begins, instantly commanding the complete attention of his listeners. "Welcome to those clans who have traveled from all over these mountains we call home to bless us once again with their company, their companionship, their lore and makings. We welcome also those pilgrims come to observe and celebrate, like we all have, the renewal of yet another cycle. The TlammaTain is a huge mountain range and it contains many peoples. We of the EthuMaahg would have it so that these mountains become a singular range united not by a common ruler, but instead, ruled by common tenants: safety, respect, decency, fellowship, tolerance, and a love of shared experiences. To those of you who have sojourned with us before, we are happy to have you with us again. For those of you who have chosen now as the first time you grace us with your presence, you have chosen well."

His voice manages to convey both a sense of lightheartedness and gravity, a trick of the acoustics involved in the construction of the space make it so that his words carry to the ends of the hall without apparent effort.

"I am here to bring you but a little diversion before the night is too far gone and the revelry takes you all. We have a special gift for you tonight, something unprecedented that may very well never be repeated again. There is a one among our youth who has an offering to submit before all you gathered here, a most unusual offering in that she is proffering to dance her Claahns'Dane for you. The Claahns'Dane is an integral part of the Ethu heritage, the ancestral war dance of our people, and no two Ethu will ever dance it the same. Up until now, we have not thought to control it, for it comes when we are in need of it.

"But some few members of our youth, influenced by the growing dance culture they have observed coming out of the Provinces, have begun experimenting with its potential. Nasiya is one such, and she would like to share it with you. Please understand how truly rarely any Ethu will share their Claahns'Dane in a public forum not made up entirely of their kin. But in the spirit of fostering more open relations between the people of this city kingdom, and others with whom we share this land, she wishes to offer this as a kind of opening of the way. Nasiya! Come grace us with your dance, with your Claahns'Dane!"

A shock of recognition runs through Kithiik and he has to exert heinous effort to keep his jaw from dropping open. The Ethu girl who steps forward from the midst of the throng is the very same girl who waylaid him on his way to the hall. Her bearing completely uncharacteristic of the Ethu he's seen so far, she sashays forward with an insouciant swagger, a deliberate sass in her steps. Affecting an almost challenging air, she takes a long look around, surprising a mortified Kithiik by looking right at him and winking ostentatiously before settling into a wide stance at the open center of the hall. She seems happy to have discomfited him, judging by the half smile visible on her face before she closes her eyes and settles into a profound stillness. Nothing seems to happen for well nigh a minute. Time stretches, the silence remains undisturbed.

A hush lies over the space like a blanket of waiting. Holding the attention of the entire room hostage, Nasiya stands unmoving in the grip of a stillness so complete, the first time her hands twitch her audience perceives it like a visual claxon, proclaiming the return of life to an otherwise inanimate statue. She begins to clench her fingers, ever so slowly, and with that clenching comes a shift in the collective energy of the space.

Kithiik chances a look around, notices that the Ethu have all closed their eyes and appear deeply engaged in intense contemplation. The atmosphere thickens, turning turgid and expectant, building with an upwelling of unseen pressure. Her fingers, rigid and clawed, flex closer to a closed fist and he can see that she struggles with something now. In the set of her jaw, the minute shaking at her wrists, lie the visible clues to the tumult going on inside her. The pressure continues to build, expanding steadily, remorselessly, and the energy of the room reflects the change.

Some of the Ethu grow restless in their meditations, allowing moans so low they're almost whimpers to escape from their pursed lips. He marks the sound of rustling clothing and lightly clinking chimes as many of them subtly shift their positions without ever opening their eyes.

At the center, Nasiya still holds the room captive, seeming to encompass the entire collective energy of the space within the clench of her clawed fingers. A vein pulses upon her forehead, her visage intent and focused utterly inward. A span of several seconds more, and a feral grin splits her lips. Her jaw muscles work as she gnashes her teeth behind the skin of her cheeks.

The assembled Ethu, though still obviously concentrating and closed-eyed, release a chorus of moans. Admiring grins blossom across their countenances, more than a few of them looking every bit as strained as the female in the middle of the space. The human spectators can only look on in complete non-understanding, conscious only of a momentous something happening right before their eyes but unable to interpret any of it —all save Kithiik. Nasiya's fingers are almost closed into a fist, the tension of the room reaching unbearable proportions. She attempts to turn her face upward, toward the tree dome above her, but she moves ever so slowly, ponderously, as if her head has inexplicably doubled in weight, the tendons of her neck tight and ridged with effort.

In the long seconds between when she begins to move her head, and when she finally manages to complete the action, allowing the collective energy of the room to spill over and burst through the psychic dams constructed for it, Kithiik feels the faintest tingling at a familiar place in the middle of his chest, and the slightest pressure at his groin. The tingling spreads, radiating outward from those two points like a set of cymbals struck by an invisible hand. The sensation cycles through him, swiftly growing in intensity, building toward a moment of translation.

He closes his eyes as the Ethu have done, and almost immediately the tingling transmutes into an exquisite series of sounds both heard and felt throughout his body entire; ripples of increasingly rhythmic vibrations fade into his awareness like a revelation's slow dawning. Already gathered within the invisible grip of Nasiya's clenched fingers, a storm of strength and power roils, waves forming a symphony of striking tones, rich with blazing life, each subtly different than the one before it, every chord struck eliciting a sympathetic reverberation he feels in his flesh and bones.

The patterns play upon his physical—elements of the feral, notes of defiance in the rhythms lance through his chest and touch his heartbeat, trigger the warrior in him; blatant carnal joy and violence inlaid like finely set gems in the interwoven tapestry of physical sound bolt through his lower belly, his groin. The intensity as the pattern builds is close to painful so acutely does it affect every cell of his being. His body and consciousness sing with the fiery, brilliant exultation of her orchestra. He can feel the strangely distinct, fabulously intricate melody of her rhythms pulsing everywhere from the tips of his fingers to the soles of his feet, ebullient and triumphant. An expression of the purest, most beautiful joy transfigures his face, and the beginnings of tears well up in his eyes.

Then Nasiya releases the tide.

Her face finally turns toward the ceiling of the great hall, the gathered Ethu poise upon the edges of an unseen precipice, the atmosphere of the space so swollen with pressure and expectation it feels like it must fly apart at any second. She stretches her mouth wide in a yawning, straining, silent scream.

The multitude of Ethu loose a slow building shout in her stead, rising in volume, giving voice to the wail she withholds. She raises her rigidly tensed arms and clawed hands above her head in direct proportion to the swelling utterance of the collective howl, and her body shakes in seizure-like spasms as the energy peaks. When the shout reaches its wailing crescendo, humans and Ethu alike caught up in the outcry, her eyes rip open and she unleashes the pent up potential in a savage tumult of sudden and explosive movement that almost beggars description.

To the end of his days, Kithiik will have a hard time describing what he saw that night to any who weren't there. All his efforts at trying to explain the atmosphere in the hall will continually result in failure. Those watching, human and Ethu alike, shouted aloud at the completion of a particularly beautiful motion,

cried out, stomped their feet, slammed their hands down on tables at her spinning passage as if compelled to voice the visceral nature of their appreciation.

His description will not do her performance justice when he says Nasiya threw her body into some of the most complex maneuvers he's ever seen with a speed that snatched his breath away. There are moments when she seems to blur, spinning as nothing human can spin, repeatedly lashing out with all her limbs one after the other, slashing at the air like a living blade, moving through space as if buoyed upon invisible currents. She catapults herself into somersaulting, flying kicks, landing on tables, rebounding off the backs of chairs, never spilling a bowl, nor knocking over a single dish, light footed as any spirit.

Gradually, she slows, and he notes the innate grace of her people shining forth from every movement. When finally she throws back her head and arms, bringing them round in the loveliest trajectory, her body first arcing then bending like a drawn bow, arms windblown boughs on a slender tree, fingers trailing branches coming to rest around her knees like a wrapped prayer, he almost weeps.

The room, and he with it, goes berserk.

A raucous, thundering din of shouting, clapping, whooping, cheering, stomping madness overtakes the room and everyone in it. Men and women leap out of their seats and off their benches as if catapulted; Ethu from tables at the higher tiers scramble and swing and drop to floor level at dizzying speed, all converging on the central space and the young Ethu girl waiting there, triumphant and flushed and brilliantly alive. Half a dozen of the fastest Ethu to meet her sweep her into their arms, pass her from embrace to embrace, all of them weeping and laughing and screaming with the sheer joy of the moment. Those on the outer rings of the convergent circle, caught up in the moment but without the outlet of access to the source of it all, turn their ecstatic energies on one another, embracing fiercely, passionately, clapping each other on the backs, clasping wrists and striking up little dances in the midst of the throng.

Music suddenly fills the night, pipes, drums and tambourines adding their collective input to the sound. Somewhere on the outskirts of that crazed floor, surrounded by revelers in various

states of celebration, Kithiik's table sits dazed and slightly incredulous in a mini-island of its own, everyone present rocked to their core by what they've just experienced. Across from Kithiik, Shunkerr seems almost bewildered with awe, nonplussed at the extent of impact on his very being. Stoic Duhmane sits there also, a smile transforming his forbidding countenance into something slightly less ominous looking. He, at least, appears completely unsurprised but thoroughly thrilled all the same. Di'aahna has disappeared from her place beside Kithiik, joined in the spontaneous revelry out in the middle of that space somewhere. Malaas, for her part, still sits opposite him, an emotional admixture Kithiik cannot entirely place fills her eyes when she finds
his.

This makes sense to him, for in the aftermath of what feels like a miracle, he hasn't the faintest clue exactly what to think or feel. Some part of him almost shies away from the effulgent splendor of the memory. He's pretty positive no one experienced Nasiya's dance quite the way he did, at least not among the human onlookers. Di'aahna and Wheirdaahn both have named him a Sensitive, and though he possesses no real idea of what that entails, he's beginning to think it might mean beautiful things.

"How did she do that? Is it thauma? Where did these people come from?" Although he speaks rhetorically, not really expecting an answer, he receives one anyway. Duhmane's medium low rumble effortlessly pierces the surrounding din to reach Kithiik's ears.

"They are an Elder race, meaning they were here before any of our people. No one knows how they do what they do, and typically, no one gets to see it in such spectacular fashion. First the ChimeSong of their clan and then an actual demonstration of the Claahns'Dane; you should consider yourself extremely blessed by whatever gods you worship, for you may never experience the like again.”

Kithiik dazedly looks up at the hunchback.

“But she pulled something to her, collected something from the very air or some such. All the Ethu were affected. What was she doing? What was she gathering?”

Again, Duhmane’s steady voice parts the clamor like a curtain.

“What you felt was the energy of their Claahns’Dane. It is not a phenomenon easily understood or explained and it would probably be best discussed under different circumstances. Perhaps we shall speak of it on the morrow.

For now, I recommend that you record all that you can of these moments, place the memories in a box somewhere inside of you, and do not lose them for they are priceless.”

At this unexpectedly poignant sentiment, Shunkerr rouses from his introspection. “If you would not mind, I would very much like to take part in that conversation on the morrow. There is much I do not understand, and my interest is piqued beyond measure. If you will excuse me, I think I shall take my leave now. I have much to think on, and the night and celebration are getting on. I would rather spend my remaining waking hours in contemplation of the remarkable experiences of this evening. I may very well have to procure a new journal before this journey sees its end. I would ask if any of you would like to join me in a night of scholarly retrospection, but I fear I already know the answer to that question. Therefore, I shall leave it unasked. I bid you all good night.”

With no further words the scholar collects himself, slowly rising from his seat at the bench. As he proceeds to leave the hall, cocooned within a reverie so deep that revelers almost unconsciously make way for his passage, Kithiik slightly shifts his opinion of the man. If Shunkerr's acerbity can be skewered by beauty, then the scholar is human after all and not solely composed of judgments, scrolls and scribing. Kithiik cannot entirely blame him either. If he had a journal, he'd probably be extremely tempted to write in it himself on a night like this, even if all that came out was gibberish. He might actually have to pursue that later.

Still thronging with revelers, the escalating celebration palpably changes the energy of the space, raising it up a notch into the fete that will ultimately carry the rest of the night. It is infectious. He can feel himself being called to join in with that energy, to perhaps try his hand at dancing for the first time or some other such lunacy he'll probably fiercely regret come the morrow. A warm body settles itself beside him and Kithiik realizes he's been immersed in his own reverie for a moment longer than a moment. Malaas has come around and seated herself next to him and Duhmane has disappeared, perhaps succumbing to the revelry and allowing himself to be swept away somewhere within that ongoing celebration. Kithiik puts his back to the table as well, and he and Malaas stare out into the open middle of the hall together, sitting close, thighs touching, arms brushing, the familiar tension a suddenly live, jittering thing between them.

"That girl winked at you before she started. Is that her? Is that the girl I tasted on your lips, the one who wants to meet me?"
He turns to her with a grin. "Uh huh. I still can't believe it. Can you believe it?" An answering grin, delightful in its open wickedness, spreads across her face. "No, I can't. But, yes, I'm really looking forward to it."

His mouth goes dry. Again. He has a chance to wonder if that will ever change before she kisses him. He can sense her near-constant, underlying hunger even when her lips are playful, teasing. He can feel it in the feverish writhing of her tongue twining round his, the abandoned way she throws herself into the kiss. Within seconds she climbs atop him, straddling his lap and hungrily devouring his face. Her hair falls round his head in a frizzy halo; her hands at the back of his head pull him deeper into the avid exploration of her wanting mouth. Her lips are everywhere. She has hiked the rich fabric of her dress up her thighs to straddle him; one leg completely exposed as the slit makes of it an offering.

He takes the palms of his hands along the smooth toned skin of her legs, traces a slow line up and under the rich folds of fabric, brings his hands to rest on either ass cheek as she moves upon him, wishing she were riding him, cradling her in both hands. She nips his upper lip, tugs at his lower, licks his face. Playing while she plays, he spreads her cheeks beneath her skirt—she's gonna stain his brand new leggings. "Right now." She says it breathy, her voice lower by an octave than usual, irises almost glazed over with need.

"Here?" He still doesn't know the customs, isn't quite sure of what will step over the bounds.

"Right. Now."

She says it again, this time shoving a hand between them and down, pulling at the ties on the front of his leggings, looking him in the eyes as she does it, daring him to stop her.

The moment recalls shades of his fever dream, only he's not dreaming, and this time she is intent on having him all the way inside. He's never been all the way inside her. She's teased and taunted him, even ridden the tip of his phallus to orgasm, but he's yet to feel what it's like to bury himself within her up to his balls, to listen to her gasp as he thrusts into her as deeply as he can possibly go.

She pulls him free and presses the length of his cock up along his stomach, leaning into him to hide its presence from the rest of the room, filling his mouth with her tongue, his senses with the smell of her hair, the feel of her voluptuous weight atop him, the slow, anticipatory grind of her hips as she shifts position. She adjusts one last time, raising herself just enough to allow him entry, eyes locked on his own.

"I told you I'd have you inside me."

And she slides down his cock, wrapping her arms around his head, pressing her forehead to his, holding his gaze as her eyes widen and her breath comes in pants. It's a slow descent, and she doesn't stop until her pussy lips rest in his pubic hair, his phallus sheathed entirely by her heat, tightly gripped in the soaking wet flesh of her cunt. They sit like that for a moment, eyes closing for a long second in sighing, mutual acknowledgement of delicious pleasure, foreheads resting together.

He remembers his hands as if coming back from a dream, a myth of his life wherein all he needed was eyes and a cock; rediscovers them just as the music he's temporarily forgotten changes tempo. Her ass is still in his palms, as is the weight of her flesh, the power to flex his fingers and spread her cheeks apart beneath the hiked folds of her dress. Watching her eyes fly open, he feels her fingers dig into the back of his neck as he pulls her forward, further onto him, celebrates the grunts pushed out of his mouth and into hers. He welcomes her lips when she leans forward to swallow his face, tempted to keep his eyes open during the kiss, dueling with her tongue. She bites his lip when he pushes up into her again, opens her mouth, grits her teeth, and pushes back.

Glorious.

The music swirls around them, the pace quickening, tone picking up yet another notch, the sounds of revelry feeling like an accompaniment to their coupling, a raucous encouragement. Kithiik cannot help but let a wide smile spread across his features. Here he sits in the middle of a banquet hall, cock buried in the cunt of a delectably beautiful woman, miles and miles away from death's door. She sees his smile and grins an answer, fastening her hands round the back of his neck and letting her hips start to work like no one is watching. His new leggings are going to be hopelessly stained. He apperceives the veiled challenge in her stare, in the twist of her lips when she grits her teeth and grinds down onto him, watching his eyes glaze.

Something stirs in him, answering the call of the creature behind her irises, flexing with expansive swiftness from its hiding place within him. With only a feral turn of his grin as warning, he reaches up behind her neck, grabs a fistful of curly hair in one hand and pulls sharply down. The gasp he receives is like the music already in his ears: heady, intoxicating in a way he can't explain. The increased arch of her spine, the jut of her gorgeous breasts, the subtle body language bespeaking acquiescence even as she fucks him all the harder, all fit as separate parts of a symphony he has only just begun to recognize.

His fist in her hair triggers an instant response; immediately her hips kick into overdrive and he feels the culmination coming. He can see her lips moving, just barely hear her voice over the music and reveling; a constant, panting stream part moan, part speech, face pointed toward the treed roof of the hall. Drawing her closer with his free arm, he snatches one plump nipple into his mouth, taking it between his teeth through the fabric of her dress, biting hard enough to make her squeal. The pressure builds in him, and he can feel her orgasm approaching at speed, signaled by clutch and spasm, squeeze and quiver, his cock pulsing in rhythmic agreement as she rides him. She pulls her head forward and he lets go his grip of her hair. Taking his head in both her hands, she looks him squarely in the face, talking into his lips.

"Fuck! Yes. Oh gods, you feel…every bit as good as I knew you would." The words come out in fits and starts, short gasps. Her eyes open, close, flare open again.

"I want you to come inside of me. Remember what I learned…about the Ethu herbs? …Nothing. To. Fear…" Her body suddenly goes almost rigid, her rhythm changing in an instant to a hard, grinding slowness, eyes huge in her face, shudders running the length of her. "I'm coming…oh goddess this feels so good! Fuck!"

She comes in waves, breath juddering into his mouth, riding the swells of her orgasm, hips moving in spasms, eyes clamping shut and Kithiik belatedly realizes his own orgasm is upon him. He squeezes her ass hard, with both hands, pulling her forward as far as she can go, pushing himself that much deeper, eliciting moans from the backs of both of their throats, his breath squeezing from between his teeth.

"Oh gods yes!" she groans the words, wrapping her arms around his head and panting the syllables into his ear. He barely has to move, between her weight and his grip, the feel of her sheathing him, cunt still clenching with the ripples of her orgasm, two days worth of unreleased pressure well up inside him until he fears the explosion might break something.

"Fuck. Yes. I feel it coming." Her voice in his ear, almost choked with pleasure, gasping with every undulation, sends him over whatever edge was left.

"Yes! Come inside me Kithiik. Do it now. Fuck!"

Clamping down on the flesh of her hips as anchor, desperately suppressing the insane shout that wants to rip out of his throat, he pumps himself empty inside her, his seed funneling out of him, milked by the constrictions of her cunt, the sound of his groans buried in the mounds of her breasts, drowned amidst the music. He has no idea how they must look, the two of them sitting there slumped together, draped over each other in obvious release, nor can he bring himself to care. In the middle of an open banquet hall, he sits with sides heaving, face buried in the cleavage of a woman he's seen for cycles, but only known for days, cock buried to the hilt in her sex, surrounded by reveling, and is content as he can ever remember being in all his days.

Chapter Seven
SEXY TIME

Twice now in a single night, Kithiik has engaged in a very public display of sexuality, and he's grateful for the billionth time that he's in the mountain kingdom and not in Wah'evi Towne, or any of the other Provinces for that matter. He doubts he'd be afforded the freedoms that pass for completely normal here. Malaas straddles his lap, arms round his neck, head draped upon his shoulder. He listens to the revelry going on around them and breathes in the sandalwood scent of her skin, feeling her heartbeat against his chest, his spent phallus still inside her. Eventually she stands, his penis slipping out of her in the process, and gives him room to retie his leggings beneath the concealing drape of her dress.

Since she came to him in his fever dream and rode the tip of his member to orgasm, he's fantasized about what it would feel like to be as far inside her as he could possibly manage. Now he knows, and far from sating his desire, the act itself has had the opposite effect on the both of them—they want more.

His leggings finally in presentable condition, Kithiik stands and together they take a surreptitious look around to see how much trouble they've gotten themselves into with so obvious a sexual display. Hunchbacked Duhmane is nowhere to be seen, Shunkerr left long ago, and as for the other revelers filling the rest of the hall, no one seems to take the slightest notice of them.

"I can feel your seed running down the insides of my thighs." Malaas says the words casually, the same way she would remark upon the weather. A thrill of excitement runs through Kithiik.

"I think I want to feel it all over my back next. You might

just have to take me from behind. How about it Kithiik, you good for another round?"

Bone and blade but the woman has ahold of his triggers or some such thing! At her words, his spent loins stir in a way that proclaims unmistakably his readiness for another go.

Perhaps catching him surreptitiously looking down, Malaas flashes him a smile, radiating equal parts smugness and hunger. "Let's go find someplace to play some more."

The lively music, plentiful banquet and joyous celebration in the aftermath of the demonstration make of the atmosphere a delightful thing. Though he absolutely looks forward to more with Malaas, Kithiik finds himself the tiniest bit reluctant to leave the hall just yet. He has never made time for any festivities, never given himself over to celebration of anything but winning. His world has been one of training and payoff and more training. But now, the surge of dancing, singing revelers seems to strike him in different places, awakening dormant desires to perhaps try something new. So many things are not as they were before he slipped into the Tunnels like a shade on his way to what turned out to be a rebirth in a hundred ways. Joy has taken on new meaning, new relevance; celebration no longer a thing reserved strictly for the aftermath of the arenas. Malaas scans his face for another moment before a different, brilliant kind of smile breaks across the canvas of her features like the light of snakerise.

"The music calling you? I didn't take you for a dancer, but we can go out there if you want. I may even be able to teach you a little somethin'."

She looks at his face a moment longer and her smile grows even bigger.

"Who's the shy one now, Kithiik? I've seen you in the arena. You're nasty as any blade fighter I've seen, maybe more so, but you haven't the stomach for dance?"

He averts his eyes from hers, looking out instead into the center of a hall quite suddenly become a rather terrifying place thronging with opportunities to make a complete fool of himself. Scant seconds ago he stood contemplating perhaps going out there for the first time in his life, but that was before she actually made the offer. He hasn't even had a real drink yet. As if reading his mind, Malass grabs his hand and heads straight for the banquet tables. Immediately reaching for a large wooden goblet, she fills it from one of the pitchers and turns to him, pressing it into his hands as she does so.

"Listen, this whole place is a dance floor; we don't even need to go out into the middle of the hall or anything if you don't want. But I've seen you smile more since you came back from that fever than I ever have my entire time watching you. And if the music is calling you, and we're in the middle of this beautiful place, and nobody's really paying any attention anyway, we might as well enjoy it, right?"

She pushes the goblet to his lips, "Have a drink, Kithiik, then have another one, and let's enjoy this while we can. I don't know what life will look like when we come down from this mountain but right now, I don't have to. Drink, and then dance with me, and then we'll find a place to fuck again and again until the Dawn Serpents cross the horizon."

Whatever half-hearted excuses would have come out of him die on his lips and he takes a large mouthful of the fruity, earthy mixture in the cup, swishing it round in his mouth a time or two before swallowing. Malaas takes a mouthful from the same goblet and kisses him, spilling wine into his mouth along with her tongue, kissing him deeply and sucking on his lower lip before letting go. They fill the goblet once more and empty it in the same fashion, savoring the flavor while enjoying each other's mouths, kissing all the more passionately between each swallow. The music and the liquid seem to find his bloodstream at the same time.

Kithiik has never welcomed drunkenness, much too afraid of losing control at the wrong moment to allow himself to go there. Even still, he has come close on several occasions, when drinking in celebration of one of his wins where the alcohol was masked by the flavor and snuck up on him, catching him slightly unawares and making for a quick re-estimation of whatever drink he had in front of him. The liquid now making its way into his system and mingling with his heartbeat feels nothing like drunkenness in the making. Clean and crisp, it adds sharpness to his experience, like viewing one of the crystal-clear springs of the mountains surrounding him.

Malaas seems to reach the same place at the same time, discarding the goblet on the table and taking his hand once again, she leads him through the outskirts of the crowd toward one of the many tree trunk pillars lining the hall. They do not hurry, taking their time and letting the rhythms wash over them, Malaas steering a meandering course through the human tide. He has no idea where she leads him, and does not care in the slightest, save that perhaps he'd rather not end up in the very center of this dance floor.

She stops at one of the huge pillars, a smooth tree bole that has to be at least fifteen feet in diameter, several landings for the multiple arboreal bridges traversing the hall attached to it at intervals high above them. All around them revelers of both races disport themselves, the musicians spinning strange crosses between the lively jigs of the Provinces, and darker, more primal melodies presumably of the mountain clans. The resulting mish mash creates a chaotic dance floor full of screaming, laughing, jesting peoples of disparate clans dancing a plethora of folk and tribal dances. Kithiik won't be the only one learning something new to him. This, coupled with the drink, allows him to release some of his trepidation as Malaas turns him, putting his back to the pillar.

Pushing him up against the trunk, she presses herself close, sliding her hands up along the tight-fitting fabric of his tunic, lacing her fingers behind his head, pulling his mouth down to meet hers. She guides his hands to her hips and holding them there, takes a few paces backwards. Leaning in close, she puts her delicious lips to his ear, making herself heard over the din, and the crowd, and the rhythms beating a strange tattoo into his head.

"This one's called the Plucked Sister, watch my feet, do as I do. But remember to listen first to the music. Hear the beats? Imagine you're pacing an opponent, but you have to step on rhythm, on beat, to match him."

Malaas begins to move as she speaks, keeping his hands at her waist, slowly despite the lively tune. She matches her steps to the undertones, the spaces he begins to hear in the creases of the melody, the backbone of the music. He's stiff at first, but her metaphor of stalking an opponent opens a door, creating an association he wouldn't have come to on his own. It helps. So does she.

Beneath his hands, her voluptuous hips move in ways he's pretty sure aren't included in the traditional teaching of the Plucked Sister. It throws him off for a second, but she only laughs and corrects his step, kissing him first. They move that way for a time, her lips rewarding him between missteps, her hands running playful circuits up and down his arms, behind his neck, along his chest.

After several minutes, when the tune changes, she backs up and starts to show him a different dance, this one not as close, but a lot more lively and fun in a different way. Both of them are smiling and laughing and when he bumps into her again, this time steadily watching her feet for the next step and thereby missing his cue, she takes his face in her hands and pours herself into a lascivious kiss that lands his back against the same pillar, and her breasts pressing against his chest. Molding herself to him she guides his hand into the high slit at the side of her dress, pressing his fingers into the smooth, yielding flesh of her buttocks.

"Dance lessons over." She says with the smile he's getting used to seeing, "I want you inside me again, and you want to give it to me, so we need to go."

Kithiik looks around the hall, scanning for the nearest interesting looking exit when something tugs at his attention halfway across the hall. A ways off to the side, Di'aahna stands with a small mixed group of Ethu, humans and hybrids just beginning to ascend a spiraling staircase leading to one of the many tiers spanning the hall. It takes him a second to realize she's been trying to get their attention unobtrusively and another moment to figure out why. She's communicating with no words again, speaking through her eyes in that manner he still hasn't become entirely used to.

Come here, both of you. I'll explain when you get here. This is gonna be fun. Sure he's received her message, she turns and begins walking up the stairs with the others. He grins and immediately starts toward the staircase, taking Malaas's hand and keeping his eyes on Di'aahna, weaving through the throng with half a bounce in his step, the drink singing through his system and carrying him with it.

In the midst of navigating his meandering way to the staircase, Kithiik catches a fleeting view of Duhmane halfway across the hall in the opposite direction, engrossed in close conversation with an exceptionally beautiful Ethu woman. The hunchback intrigues him, presenting a multitude of seeming contradictions, but that enigma can definitely wait for another time.

Following the group Di'aahna has attached herself to presents very little challenge. They travel slowly, laughing, talking, teasing and touching the whole while. The contact sparks Kithiik's interest, appearing to his eyes like a game of glancing touches. The subtle sexuality implicit in the surreptitious caresses and the seemingly uncontrived manner their limbs graze each other creates an amorous version of the dance the speaker performed at the outset of the evening. When he and Malaas finally catch up to Di'aahna, she drops back a step to fill them in as they go, interposing herself between their bodies and pulling them close on either side of her. She speaks softly; they perforce have to lean in to hear her almost whispered words. "There's rooms set aside that are used for…doing things." Her grin is eloquent in the extreme. "No one who isn't invited is welcome. Thanks to the two of you, we've all been invited."

Her uncovered thigh brushes Kithiik's through the fabric of his leggings. Her arm slides around his back, encircling his waist as they continue on through half-open corridors and over short bridges roofed by foliage, wrapped by branches. Surprised giggles punctuate their passage, the sounds of murmured speech come from slightly ahead. Kithiik lets his arm hang low across Di'aahna's back, fingers playing with the bottoms of her ass cheeks beneath the line of her corset, feeling the flesh shift with every step. Di'aahna squeezes her hand down into the back of his leggings, letting her fingers rest on his ass, gripping him every so often. Her other arm around Malaas, she kisses her as they walk, in a greeting that leaves all three of them stumbling, softly laughing, now more completely a part of the group, absorbed into the sensuality of the moment without having given conscious thought to it.

After a time, they come upon a series of hanging vines blocking the path, and they watch as those ahead of them simply

continue on through the curtain. Following suit, they find themselves in a scene out of some chronicler's fantasy tale. The room is a womb of sorts, partially open to the skocean above, walls made of branches seemingly grown into shape, and then covered with the most springy, sumptuous mosses and lichens to create comfortable landings no matter where one ends up. The floors are another kind of moss, the entire space filled with low pallets and beds of branches stuffed with leaves and layered with mats and grown moss covers of differing colors. The silvery light of the glimmer fish peeks through the floral curtain in places, their light augmented by the subtly glowing ambiance of phosphorescent lichens grown in cunning shapes to look like woven tapestries hung about the walls. Very near to the entrance, a narrow arboreal waterfall cascades quietly down from an unseen height above, gathering in a small pool before becoming a stream bisecting the room and disappearing into the base of one of the walls.

Close to thirty beings of mixed races recline throughout the room in various states of repose and copulation. Individuals and couples from the group peel off in differing directions as they walk through the curtain, hailed by a friendly chorus of greetings. The sound of trickling water mingles with soft cries of those in the midst of coitus. Twined limbs of varying hues make slow moving sculptures of bodies, tattoos forming patterns within patterns, the bells woven into thick locks add tinkling accompaniment to the visual song.

Awed, Kithiik turns to Di'aahna and whispers, "Please remind me to ask you what gods you worship, for surely they smile upon us like none other has in my whole life."

She meets his wide-eyed gaze with a wonder-filled look of her own, obviously just as taken aback as he, and nods her head in the affirmative before returning her attention to the tableau before them.

It is Malaas who breaks the spell, moving toward the tiny waterfall and the pool beneath it, gently pulling Di'aahna and

Kithiik with her as she goes. Cupping her hands in the pool, she takes several swallows of the water before bathing her face. She is beautiful then, an ageless vision reenacted thousands of times, in a hundred different lands.

Kithiik wonders how many men before him have been momentarily entranced by the simple sight of a bathing woman. He doesn't know what's happening to him, but if he's not careful, he thinks he may find himself wandering the path of one of the itinerant poets, expounding upon the beauty of small things in town squares for coin. Ha! The thought brings a smile to his face, and Malaas chooses that moment to look up at him. She rakes him with an answering smile absent of innocence; like a physical thing, it travels his body and returns to his eyes hungrier than before.

His body responds with an alacrity that is slightly astounding, cock hardening beneath the fabric of his leggings almost painfully fast. Rising from the edge of the pool, she takes both his hand and that of Di'aahna, pulling them to a particularly comfy looking spot in the room a short distance from the spring. They all remove their shoes, burying their toes in the spongy moss of the mat, standing in a loose circle.

"Di'aahna," Malaas says quietly, not looking at her, but staring at Kithiik instead. "Did you know that his seed is drying on the insides of my thighs right now?"

Now it is Di'aahna's turn to grin, her expression every bit as mischievous as Malaas's was hungry. Kithiik can only look on and marvel at the growing confidence of this girl woman before him, once so shy, now rapidly becoming wholly other.

"Reeeeaaallly…" purrs Di'aahna, her teeth prominently displayed within the frame of her grin, "maybe I should taste his seed, see what his flavor is like when it's mingled with yours."

"Mmmm, that does sound like a tasty idea." All three of them turn at the interruption to see a lissome figure sauntering through the twilight of the chamber. Her husky voice sends a rill of excitement through Kithiik's spine. Her eyes find his and lock onto them, a complicated mix dancing within them, strains of the song of her soul spilling out of his memory to color her approach almost godlike.

"You told me I'd get to meet her. You didn't tell me there were two." Momentarily tongue tied, Kithiik finds himself feeling more than a little star struck for the first time in his life.

"You…" he manages, just before she swallows his voice and any further words with a ridiculously salacious kiss that forcefully co-opts his thoughts, immediately shifting them to carnal places. She pulls back and turns to Malaas and Di'aahna.

"When this beautiful boy told me he wasn't alone, I told him I wanted to meet you. I am Nasiya, and your suggestion sounds about as lovely as anything I've heard all night. If neither of you mind, I would so love to join you in tasting his seed on your luscious thighs. What's your name?"

"Malaas." Visibly taken aback as much as Kithiik by the appearance of this Ethu in particular, Malaas answers with more than a hint of her old shyness suddenly in evidence. She, like Kithiik, finds it hard to take her eyes off the being before them.

"Malaas. I like that name, pleased to meet you. And you, healer, what's your name? Your calling fairly sings off you like a choir."

"I am Di'aahna, and it is so perfect to meet you in this way, at this time. You were amazing tonight, and we don't have to go over it now, but I was struck to my core by whatever you did earlier. We all were."

A huge grin spreads across the Ethu's face and her chin raises slightly, pride all over her countenance as she receives the genuine praise. Eyes sparkling, grin still adorning her features, she laughs a little laugh and spontaneously hugs Di'aahna in thanks.

"Sooo," she drags the word out, turning her attention back to Malaas, "shall we partake?"

"Oh yes please!"

Kithiik isn't even sure which girl answered but, as one, both Nasiya and Di'aahna kneel and begin to lick the insides of Malaas's thighs while she holds the folds of her dress out of their way. Kithiik is riveted to the spot. Here are not one, but three, beautiful women, one of them not even entirely human, not human at all actually, engaging in an act that would scandalize most everyone he's ever met. Two women licking his spent seed off the thighs of a third; three different skin tones, two different races, one filament of sensuality binding them all.

In the muted light of the glimmer fish high above and the hanging phosphorescent tapestries on the walls, Kithiik stands gaping at the look of disbelieving pleasure on Malaas's face, gazing down upon the two gorgeous creatures giving worship at the altar of her flesh. He can tell the exact moment one of their tongues finds her sex because her expression changes just that quickly. Her eyes close slowly, her head lolls backward on her neck, and she sways ever so slightly, like a tree caught in the very beginnings of a windstorm. Kithiik has been admiring her lips ever since he came out of his fever and now is no exception. Luscious, full, as if they were made for pleasure, as if their purpose in life is to bring joy to eyes and mouths and flesh and fingers, they part slightly to allow the egress of her silent exhale.

Like a hound following the trail of that invisible breath,

Kithiik lets his sight travel down from her lips, over the voluptuous swell of her ample breasts, nipples covered only by the rich, thin fabric of her dress, down the inviting curves of her stomach and hips, to the hands and heads of the two delectable beings currently working her into a place of extremity. Di'aahna and Nasiya move together as if they've known each other for cycles, working in harmony to bring Malaas to orgasm. Knowing smiles adorn their faces, lips randomly part in grins and tiny giggles as they take turns using their fingers and mouths to pull her closer to the brink. Kithiik watches as Nasiya turns it up a notch, burying her face in Malaas's crotch, suckling greedily at her clit. Malaas moans a little louder, twining her fingers in Nasiya's thick locks, holding her head in place as she begins to shudder.

This last triggers Kithiik right out of the role of spectator. Cock raging beneath the constraining fabric of his leggings, he steps closer to the trio, bending to whisper into Di'aahna's ear before moving around behind Malaas. Pulling his laces loose in less than seconds, he frees his stiffness from the confines of his clothing. His senses are galvanized, little things registering, leaping out as if in bass relief against a fantastic erotic backdrop: the fabulous mane of untamed, curly brown black hair above brown shoulders; the exposed channel of her spine between shoulder blades beneath the thin straps supporting the dress; rolling folds of luxurious green fabric hiked up over beautifully rounded hips; the lines of her spread thighs, the sound of a shuddered breath. The head of his cock twitches in anticipation. Bending, he snatches the dangling back hem of her dress up over her ass, catching a glimpse of a grinning Nasiya scrambling to one side in the process. Before Malaas has a clear idea of what is happening, he is grasping her by the hips, guiding his cock unerringly to the thoroughly lubricated passage of her sex, and sheathing his length in her pussy as deeply as their bodies will allow.

Malaas comes the instant his cock is inside her, already brought to the brink by the probing tongues and fingers of Nasiya and Di'aahna. Her moans become cries as he begins thrusting. Her cries become wails and she goes to her knees, body convulsing with multiple orgasms.

He drops to his knees with her, sinking to the spongy floor, gripping her hips as fulcrum, riding the ripples of her clenching cunt, grinding his hips against her buttocks, pushing his cock into her deeper and deeper. Her wails run together in a semi-mindless utterance of pleasure and invective, swearing and curses blended into the wordless stream, pushed well beyond the bounds of her first orgasm, body wracked by repeated spasms.

She finds purchase between the pillows on the mossy floor with her fingers, pushes her face and breasts into the cushions, arches her back and meets him with everything she has. The sound of their flesh smacking fills the open chamber. Sweat stands out in beads across the working muscles of his chest and stomach. His arms flex with pulling her back into him, cock filling cunt, teeth clenched, bared feral, exalting in the freedom of it.

She has told him several times she wanted to be taken. He never quite heard the words aright until this moment. Her pussy constricts continually around the length of his pulsing shaft and for a moment, the world contracts around him: the flesh gripped in his fingers; the feel of her ass cheeks hitting his pelvis; the sight of the ripples every time he impacts; the sound of her cries as she comes again and again. He slows only when he senses she has begun to reach the threshold where pleasure might shift into something other. Doesn't know how he knows, doesn't bother to question, just matches his rhythm to the clenching of her cunt, using it to gauge when to cease his movements altogether.

It is an effort of will to come back to himself, to slow with the subsiding of her internal muscles, because the rod of his sex is still unsated, still raging with an almost unbearable rigidity. Di'aahna crawls up Malaas like some erotically soothing cat, kneading and massaging, licking the sweat from her shoulder blades, making her way across the expanse of her back to the ripe flesh of her still raised buttocks. But Nasiya rivets his attention as she crawls toward him on hands and knees when he slides his sex out of Malaas.

Vividly hungry, aroused beyond telling by the spectacle she just witnessed, Nasiya has eyes only for his cock as it emerges and does not wait before taking him into her mouth. He groans aloud when she sucks him in, and she moans in sympathy, as if he fills her elsewhere by filling her mouth. She is thorough with her tongue, laving the entirety of his shaft with avid attention, moving up and down its length with consummate skill. For a moment, Kithiik can only sit back on his heels and groan, looking down on Nasiya's vine-festooned back, watching as her head bobs up and down over his cock. But Malaas awoke an animal in him, and at present, Nasiya's skilled lips round his sex are not enough to quell the driving hunger pushing outward from inside him. He wants to feel her body pressed against his, her flesh in his fingers, to bury himself in her cunt and feel the ripples as she contracts around him.

Taking gentle handfuls of her locks in both hands, he tries to ease her off him, but she will have none of it, clamping his buttocks in a fierce grip and speeding her pace as she drives his cock into her mouth again and again. His groans become louder and he finds himself fucking her mouth, the fistfuls of hair he would have used to extricate himself become handholds to anchor him. She moans in unison with his groans, for all the world like she is fucking him, pushing his cock to the back of her throat, sucking every inch of his shaft, milking him as if he were already in the midst of coming and she wanted to miss not a single drop. Blade and bone! He doesn't know how much longer he can hold out, but wants more than anything to be inside her when he lets go. Her mouth is a siphon, a cruel task-mistress giving him no quarter, allowing him no surcease, and his orgasm is rumbling closer at speed.

He starts to bend forward, letting his weight push down across her back, restricting some of the movement of her head. Reaching over her back as she continues to suck him, he finds the cleft of her buttocks, the wetness of her sex beneath, and immediately plunges two fingers deep inside. She gasps around his cock breaking her rhythm for the first time since she started. He leans further over her, creating better leverage, pushing his fingers even deeper, pulling them only partially out before plunging them in again without pause. Her mouth is stalled upon his shaft, moaning. It is the only way he can think of to extricate himself from the unremitting siphon of her lips and tongue and throat. She attempts to get back to her earlier rhythm, but is thwarted by his weight, and the insistence of his plunging fingers.

Now it is his turn not to let up on the rhythm. As he continues sliding his fingers in and out of her sex, once again using them as a surrogate cock with which to fuck her, she lets go of his shaft with her mouth to begin moaning in earnest, finally giving him respite from the driving rhythm that would have yanked him over the edge very shortly. Wasting no time, he sidles round until he is abreast of her, kneeling at her side, watching her spine arc as she pushes back into his fingers. She tries repeatedly to get her lips around his cock, but he denies her, increasing the tempo of his finger fucking with every attempt, forcing her closer to her peak. He pushes his aching forearm to its limits as he listens for the telltale rising octaves of her voice.

Just as her moans begin to crest, her husky voice giving

vent to longer, drawn out wails, he snatches his fingers away and pulls her onto her side, back facing him, replacing his fingers with his cock and filling her cunt completely in as smooth a motion as he can manage. Both of them emit a drawn out moan, panting and gasping in pleasure as her pelvis involuntarily undulates against him. He lifts one long leg, grasping the underside of her thigh at the crook of her knee, and proceeds to thrust into her, reveling in the feel of her pussy round his cock instead of his fingers, the heat of it, the squeeze of her sex.

Their moaning wails intermingle and she arches her spine to take it, reaching back with one hand to grip his ass, urging him on, moans growing louder and more frenzied with every passing second. Try as he might, Kithiik cannot for the life of him control his own rhythm. Once she gets him to speed up, he cannot slow down, cannot help but try to fuck her for everything he's worth. His hips buck uncontrollably, in the grip of a kind of seizure. His orgasm, having been made to wait already, rips through him within seconds, forcing his jaws wide apart in a guttural, open-mouthed roar proclaiming the strength of it, hips still pumping, fingers digging spasmodically into the flesh of her thigh while her voice rings out alongside his, orgasm to orgasm, both of them howling in a prolonged utterance of joined animal pleasure before collapsing into replete, panting satiation.

The rest of the night passes in a sensuous blur, the four of them enacting the stuff of fantasies repeatedly, only stumbling apart, aching and pleasurably sore in the dim light just before first crossing, when the growing radiance of the light serpents signals their imminent passage over the peaks. The three of them bid a sleepy goodbye to Nasiya, make their bedraggled way into the pilgrim's barracks, find their cots and summarily collapse upon them.

Chapter Eight

REVELATIONS

When Kithiik, Malaas, and Di'aahna finally wake, late into the day sometime between Second and Third Crossing, the number of Renewal Pilgrims still fast asleep on the surrounding cots in the barracks surprises them. Quite obviously, the three of them were not the only ones who celebrated until the wee hours of the morning. Kithiik immediately heads for the baths and a note from Shunkerr waits for him on his cot when he emerges, giving him instructions on where he can find both the scholar and Duhmane for their agreed upon conversation.

Sleepily agreeing to meet with the girls later, he wanders the paths until crossing beneath one of the grown archways adjacent to the Grand Hall and entering into a small, rather private clearing set back a little way from the main paths. Across the clearing from him, Shunkerr and the hunchback sit conversing in quiet tones on a bench made from a single fallen tree trunk beneath an open bower of vines and brightly colored blossoms. Shunkerr looks up from his conversation as Kithiik enters the clearing and for a wonder, actually manages a smile.

"Ahh, the young one will join us after all!" he says to Duhmane, but there is no maliciousness in his tone, only a light teasing. It seems the night has done the scholar some good, his habitual dourness taking a temporary holiday. As Kithiik approaches the men, he espies two young children, one Ethu, the other a human, playing quietly off to the side several yards away, engrossed in what looks like a game of camouflaging their hands with whatever dirt and leaves are available. He wonders if they await the hunchback.

"You look tired," says Shunkerr, " and I must admit I've already taken the liberty of pilfering the conversation you and Duhmane would have had, provided you'd been awake. I do not know if you are sufficiently present now to ask the questions you would have asked, but we have been conversing for some time and I can gladly share what I have learned in the interim at some other instance, on the journey down from the city for instance. As it stands, Duhmane was just about to take his leave, but perhaps he could be prevailed upon to answer at least one question?"

Duhmane looks steadily at Kithiik as he approaches and Kithiik ventures the first question that comes into his mind.

"What is an Elder Race? What do you mean when you say that they came here before we did?" When the hunchback answers, his rumble again seems to originate from the middle of his chest. "Well met, and afternoon to you. Of course you would choose to not only ask a single question containing its own answer, but also a query that cannot be satisfactorily answered in a terse summation. However, I will venture to at least give you a partial answer.

"The problem with queries like the one you have put forth is that more often than not, they lead to more questions instead of answers. The Elder Races are those that were here before the coming of man to this place. You may not be aware of this, but many believe mankind did not originate here, that we were brought here, or came to be here, from somewhere else entirely. There are facts which support this belief, fragments of history contained in legends here and there, but the vast bulk of resources that could serve as evidence have been rendered…let us say hard to come by.

"Of course, as with all things of this nature, invariably some hints, some testaments survive. In this case, the primary source of knowledge we have to draw upon is contained within the historic annals of races other than our own, like within the library of the Ethu for example. Their records tell of the coming of the first men as their people experienced it, recorded and passed down orally for generations until the fated meeting of Maahg the Second and the Ethu female, Thairn, a story of which, I do not doubt you have heard several versions.

"Your Shunkerr can tell you that union constitutes the only reason any written Ethu records exist at all. Maahg's folk made it a point to record the Ethu bard's stories, anything their people would recite in his folks' presence, transcribing things that had heretofore been only oral, thereby forever changing the culture of this particular clan of Ethu in the process. The library Maahg's folk subsequently created also enables seekers like myself and Shunkerr to discover new and interesting things concerning this land and our place within it. The reasons for the paucity of knowledge outside the bounds of this city are long and convoluted, entirely the design of men. Perhaps Shunkerr can be prevailed upon to fill you in on the quagmire of that story in time. At present, I must depart. There is knowledge to be gleaned and discoveries to be made. Interesting happenings are afoot, interesting indeed."

The hunchback stands and the second he moves from his seat on the bench, the children are at his side, serenely taking hold of both massive hands and beginning to pull him gently toward the path. Kithiik, still somewhat groggy from sleep and not as sharp as he could be, tries to muddle through Duhmane's meandering speech for several seconds, attempting to get at the nuggets of knowledge he knows must be contained within it, before at last giving it up as hopeless for the time being. He can take Shunkerr up on his offer of an enlightening conversation at some later time when understanding won't be so hard won.

Duhmane obviously does possess a store of knowledge worth picking his mind for, but puzzling out his obscure answers feels a bit too much like work at the moment. Kithiik does seize upon the moment to ask at least one question he doubts will have such an obtuse answer, though one can never tell with scholars. "One last question a lot simpler to answer?" Kithiik says as the hunchback and the children pass him. "The children, why do you most always travel with children?"

Duhmane gives him an unreadable look before turning away and allowing himself to be pulled from the clearing. Kithiik stares after him thinking the man will leave without answering when the hunchback's voice comes rumbling back to him.

"They calm me."

Kithiik stares after him for a few moments longer, then shares a speculative look with Shunkerr before sitting down opposite the scholar on the same bench.

"Good afternoon, Kithiik. I trust you spent the night well? It is good you have come, for we have somewhat pressing matters to discuss. I will proceed directly to the point, and I advise that you keep your voice in a low register for the things we have to speak of are sensitive subjects at the least, potentially lethal at worst."

All remnants of sleep flee from Kithiik in an instant, yet his face remains impassive, closing down almost immediately. Some internal part of him smiles grimly at how much he is learning in this lush and beautiful place. Certain lessons come with no warning, and one must either be willing to adapt or fail. This time, the scholar does not wait to gauge the reaction to his words. Indeed he presses on as if time were of the essence.

"Your life is no longer what it was before your experience skirting the realm of Death. Wittingly or no, you have stumbled into something more convoluted than you could possibly have realized. Our caravan is slated to leave early on the morrow and I have things to tell you before we do.

"Let me begin by saying that what happened to you is a rarity. You have been blessed beyond measure. Very few survive an encounter like the one you had. I trust you are more than aware of the stories surrounding those Tunnels and now I daresay you are more knowledgeable than most on the truth contained within them. As I related when first we met, I am a scholar particularly interested in a certain Elder Race. It turns out there are many who are interested in that race, a great many in fact, more than you may ever know, or care to know for that matter. What you couldn't have been aware of is that I am already a servant of the principle representative of that selfsame race. I, along with others, serve the one whom you…met…in the Tunnels."

Revelation.

Bits and pieces fall into place like the bricks of a wall carefully positioned by a mason's skilled fingers. A scant week ago Kithiik would have had his knife out and to the scholar's throat before he could so much as blink again. Now he only sits there wonderingly, mind reeling with possibilities converging.

"A cult? You're part of a cult?"

"As I said, you would be wise to keep your voice down, young man! It is old beyond your understanding. There is history between the two races, and not a pleasant one either. Somehow you, born of a backwater town at the very outskirts of civilization, without even a decent school of defense or a blade band worth mentioning, have managed to survive where so many have not. You live where countless others have died. I can only suppose that as a reward for that, your youth, exuberance and… performance, the Mistress has chosen to utilize you for a quite significant task, one of utmost importance. I understand this may be much to swallow at once, but soon, we will be down from this place, and I intend to depart shortly thereafter. It is her will that you accompany me, at least for the first leg of your journey."

Kithiik's mind stumbles like his fevered feet back in the Tunnels. So much of what he's gleaned, so much of what he thought he knew is not as it seemed.

"What makes you, or her, think I'd be willing to do anything of the kind?"

The scholar's face takes on an expression Kithiik will find himself revisiting in his memories for some time to come in later days and weeks. Staring at the scholar's pinched visage he finally realizes the source of the apparent animosity, or at least, mild disdain he's felt from Shunkerr from the very beginning. The feelings arise from a place so unexpected and so foreign, Kithiik would never have credited them outside the context the old man just gave him. Shunkerr is *jealous*, envious of Kithiik's youth and whatever enabled him to come through his ordeal with the Mistress, as he calls her, in one piece. Kithiik thinks the bulk of it had to do with having Di'aahna there at the other side, but if the scholar wishes to think more of it, Kithiik will go on letting him.

"Ahh," the scholar answers, "you have no idea how special is your case; how long it has been since any man came through the Venemaste, the Ordeal By Poison, with his wits still about him. You've been marked in a way you may not recognize, and most cannot see, but you belong to the Mistress now; she's in your blood. As for your serving her, the Mistress has no doubt of your willingness. She says…She says it is a matter of scent."

And simple as that, it is done. Kithiik will forever wonder what his life would have been like had he refused, knifed the scholar then and there and taken his chances with the aftermath. But he doesn't. The scholar sees it the minute he makes the decision, mayhap even thought it a foregone conclusion. Perhaps one day Kithiik will seek to test the Mistress again. Perhaps one day but not today. Shunkerr continues speaking almost immediately, but his slightly distracted manner and absent smoothing of his scholarly robes give Kithiik pause.

"Very well. The task she has set for you will take you deep into the Provinces if I don't miss my guess. I will only be with you for the first portion of your journey, as far as the first

Province actually. I have business to attend there."

Shunkerr seems increasingly agitated as he goes on, out of all proportion to the information he relates and suddenly, the old man's guard no longer holds quite so stoically in place. Kithiik finds himself able to read more from Shunkerr's face during these few seconds than in any other interaction thus far. The pale, wrinkled creases round the gray eyes, the sharp nose, the ingrained lines leading down from his mouth, the scowl lurking between the bushy white eyebrows, all bespeak a lifetime of diligent study, a single-minded devotion to sussing out mysteries and unlocking secrets; stories of long nights by candle light spent perusing old scrolls in even older libraries written in the folds of his skin like the pages of a book. The occasional twitch of his gray eyes, and continued smoothing of his robes make it obvious that something pressing weighs on the scholar's mind and eventually Kithiik can take it no more.

"What is it? You got questions burnin' you, I see it all over your face, scholar. You might as well get it over with."

Shunkerr lapses abruptly into complete silence, looking everywhere but at Kithiik's face, before beginning to speak in a half-babbled rush not at all characteristic of his usual semi-condescending manner. "Well, many of the histories go vague on this particular facet of the lore, so few documented cases survived, you see, but I have done extensive study in this area and the histories all allude to the fact that the Venemaste exacts certain —changes in those who survive it." No sooner have the words left Shunkerr's mouth than he cannot seem to stop staring at Kithiik, viewing him rather like one would a pinned moth, or the innards of some strange animal stretched out on an academy table for perusal.

"Perhaps you've already begun to experience some signs of this?"

Kithiik's thoughts flash immediately to the vision he

received on the plateau, the first of its like he'd ever gotten, and from there to his experience in the great hall with Nasiya and her Claahns'Dane, then the fact that Wheirdaahn and Di'aahna both have named him a Sensitive. How much to share with the old man?

"Changes? What kinds of changes? Like, have I been feelin' funny or some such?"

"No, no, not necessarily anything that would manifest itself in that way. Every Elder Race possessed an inherited thauma unique to their people. The—people of which we speak, of which the Mistress is a scion, were a very, shall we say, physical, people. Their mahj'ick dealt with the flesh: sensuality, touch, and intuition in those realms. Skills like those translated into unlikely places. It seems that some of the chosen males were not only renowned for their skills as consummate lovers, which of course was to be expected, but also as adepts in the realms of medicine. Some of them were capable of gaining penetrating insight simply from touching an afflicted patient. Sensitives they were named, but it meant somewhat different than when folk apply the term these days."

The title "Sensitive" hits Kithiik like a weight to his chest but he carefully keeps his face closed down, letting nothing slip. Last night, he did get to see another side of the scholar. Perhaps he need not maintain so hostile a guard when in his presence. Presently however, his thoughts whirl in a mental hailstorm, more and more puzzle pieces clicking into place like a second story on a bricklayer's wall. Renowned for their skills as consummate lovers, he'd said. Before the Serpentari, Kithiik had never been touched. Since then, he's done more than his share of touching, with none the wiser. Now he begins to wonder if thauma, poison, a fantastic healer and her gods have contrived to leave him with some gifts none but the Serpentari could have foreseen. Blade and bone, what twisted fortune!

"Mayhap I have felt little stirrings of change. Nothing I can put a finger on as of yet, but perhaps I might bring it to your attention if something more solid shows up." *When I trust you a little bit more.*

The old man holds his gaze steadily for a moment longer than a moment, weighing, then exhales in resignation at what he sees and continues.

"Very well. You should now at least have an inkling, some idea as to the uniqueness of your case, and how intriguing it is to one such as myself. I can only guess at how you were able to come through your encounter alive, healer or no, nor why the Mistress has chosen to start you out with a mission of such importance. But I need not know. As I'm sure you're aware, the need for secrecy is paramount. I must stress one thing: This warning is the only one you will ever receive. Compromise the tasks you are given, the agents with whom you interact, or the Mistress herself, and it will not go well for you. Her agents are everywhere, many of them aren't even aware whom they serve."

Kithiik notices movement at the edge of the clearing, turns to see Malaas standing on the path, just beneath the last of the forest canopy. His heart beats a little faster when he realizes he now has yet another secret, or even series of secrets, he's going to have to keep from those closest to him. Relationships and intimacy can create a double-edged sword. Only a month ago, he would have said but a single person lived on the face of the land whose feelings he legitimately cared about injuring. Now he can add at least two more to that number.

Shunkerr follows his gaze and notices Malaas. He continues speaking as she slowly approaches across the lush green grass of the clearing, once again dressed in her traveling clothes, light from the Serpents limning the outside of her curly mane like a halo and glinting off the chains affixed to her belt.

"All will be arranged; you need do very little in terms of

preparation." Shunkerr continues speaking as if nothing is amiss. "I suspect the wheels have already been set into motion. An opportunity will present itself before the end of the journey down the mountain, and when it comes, simply take it. It will not be easy to mistake. I shall leave you now to your musings. Perhaps there will come a time when you have questions aplenty. Once we have safely arrived in the Provinces I shall have ample opportunities to enlighten you. Until then."

Rising, he makes his way out of the clearing, only perfunctorily greeting Malaas as they pass each other. Kithiik remarks her furtive gait and the reticence of her bearing immediately, wondering at the cause. He realizes he wants her to come with him. Wherever this task takes him, he will most assuredly want the companionship of someone he can trust without question, and Shunkerr does not fit that role by a long shot. He smiles at her as she gets closer, but she returns it with only a wan smile of her own. Burdened by something, she sits next to him on the bench and looks out over the clearing. He does the same, waiting, giving her space, feeling into the silence. When she finally speaks, her voice is subdued, she stares down at her twining fingers, will not meet his eyes.

"What did my uncle tell you?"

One question, no more than six words, and a weight the size of a small boulder forms in the pit of his stomach. He looks at her sharply, but she still refuses to meet his eyes. He tries dissembling.

"Nothing to do with you, if that's what you're worried about. He revealed no sordid truths you'd want no one to know about."

"Actually," she answers, finally looking up at him, more nervous, more vulnerable than he can ever remember seeing her look, "actually, I think he did."

He is recoiling before he can think, flying off the bench away from her as if suddenly discovering she's poisonous; finds himself on the ground, backpedalling, his head shaking in constant denial the entire time.

"Kithiik, don't look at me like that! Do not judge me until you have at least heard me out! Please?"

The stricken look on her face cuts him to his marrow, cleaving deeper than he would have thought possible. Again an emotional admixture wars for dominance across the canvas of her face: fear, a measure of defiance, anger, need. But what is he to think? How to take this? Malaas? An agent of the Serpentari; a member of a cult he's not even heard the glimmer of until just this moment? How did this come to be?

"Don't judge me until you have heard me out." She says it again, a measure of steel asserting itself beneath the words now, a growing conviction stopping the wringing of her hands and changing the tone of the entire exchange. One emotion slowly comes to dominate the palette of her face, and surprisingly enough, it looks a lot like defiance. Her expression pulls him out of his spin, grounding him in the possibility that he is in over his head; that perhaps this puzzle holds more pieces than he could ever have imagined.

Focus. Hear her out. Let her tell her story, figure out how to proceed from there. He refuses to look at her as he brings himself under a semblance of control. Nonetheless the power of her gaze sears his flesh, her wordless entreaty to be heard no less compelling for its silence. Pulling himself together by what feels like a supreme effort of will, he finally relents, looking up at her from beneath hooded lids. He gives her the barest of nods from behind his involuntarily closed down face, not trusting himself to move from where he has come to rest on the grass of the clearing. He waits and listens, unsure of how to react, unsure of how he feels, unsure of anything, hoping against hope that something in the story she has to tell him will redeem what feels like a massive betrayal. He's not even sure what she has betrayed, only that it does indeed look and feel that way at the moment.

Seeing that she has his attention finally, that he's quieted his inner voices for the moment, she looks down at her hands and begins to speak, her voice quiet, her words somehow all the more piercing because of it. "What do you know of the Provinces? You go by what you've heard from people who've been there: merchants, mercenaries and caravan guards who've traveled between them. I was born in the Provinces. Being a girl there isn't nearly so desirable as being a boy, not nearly. I was brought to Wah'Ehvi very young, but not before seeing things I wish I had never seen, things I only barely escaped having done to me. I've yet to actually meet the Mistress, but I have met her Daughters, one of them anyway. She's the one who taught me the way of the hammered chain."

At his startled reaction, she allows the faintest hint of pride to show, evident in the set of her head, the burning of her eyes. The hammered chain is a weapon he knows very little about, save for how rarely one encounters a wielder, and the extraordinary difficulty in mastering it. Another piece of the puzzle clicks into place and his eyes fly to the broad belt she wears even now, festooned with weaponry hidden in plain sight. He wonders which of them she actually wields.

"Yeah, Kithiik, I know how to use that weapon now, mine is familiar to me as your blades are to you. But tell me, when was the last time you saw a woman who knew how to wield any weapon at all? When was the last time you saw a female keeper of law, or member of a blade band? We can't even think about applying to a school of defense unless we're born or married into one of the noble families, and I wasn't about to go to an academy. Our realities are different from yours. You probably never even notice the disparities.

You hear the stories about the well-meaning ones, the honorable men who are constantly pledging themselves to

'protect' those that are 'weaker'. But does it ever occur to anybody that maybe if they put weapons in our hands and quit treating us like we're weaker, things would be different?"

151

Once again Kithiik finds himself in a position where everything he thought he knew has been turned sideways. His entire world seems to keep transforming in front of his very eyes. Every time he thinks he's got ahold of it, some other fundamental something goes and rearranges itself. He's never given the absence of female keepers, or members of blade bands, or caravan guards, or pretty much any martial post a second thought. It is the natural way of things, isn't it? But a woman who's been through infinitely more than he ever would have guessed sits in front of him at this very moment, and she would definitely disagree.

Malaas continues her narrative, less contrite with every passing second, less apologetic, more impassioned, angry, giving vent to feelings she only rarely voices aloud. She speaks quietly, intensity and passion twining her words, lending them strength, conviction.

"I've witnessed disgusting things I hope to never see again, and I learned the chain so no man could ever do to me so casually what I've seen them do to others. The Stone Daughter gave me the means. The cult put the skill at my fingertips, not anyone else. They taught me to see how lopsided our treatment is, though I'd already seen enough to need precious little coaxing. For me, the promise of training was all I needed to hear. I'd have done just about anything to get my hands on a weapon, to be trained in its use. Serving the Mistress didn't even give me pause. I do not rue the bargain, nor do I think I ever will."

She is looking him directly in the eye by the time she finishes, daring him to contradict any of her experience, challenging him to find fault with her decisions. He cannot, and secretly, he is glad. Instead of speaking, potentially fumbling the moment with botched attempts at articulation, he rises, coming to sit beside her on the bench. The greenery of the surrounding forest, rich and lush beneath the light of third crossing, the glimmering radiance of the light serpents filtering down through the shallows of the floating lake above them, make of the bower a beautiful place, luminous and shadow-filled simultaneously.

The birds native to these forests sing their strange songs in the trees, and it seems the perfect place for healing. Kithiik is reminded of the deep and unlikely belly laugh that comes pouring out of Di'aahna, the sound of which possesses a healing quality all its own, instantly infectious and effortlessly shifting moods into brighter places. Malaas never takes her eyes off him, nor does her expression soften until he leans in to kiss her on the eyelids one by one. He has never kissed anyone on the eyelids, doesn't know why he does so now save that he follows an impulse speaking sense to him from somewhere he need not question. Perhaps moments like these fall within the scope of the changes Shunkerr spoke of, Kithiik doesn't know and can't say he cares. He knows only that the rigidity melts from her frame as his lips rest upon her lids, and he realizes she was holding her breath. Strong as she is, his rejection would have cut deep, though she may not know it would have hurt him almost as much. She takes a deep breath and lets it out again, allowing the tension to leech out of her with the exhale, putting her hands to his cheeks, tracing the lines of his face.

"Thank you."

Part of the released breath, the sentiment passes into him through his skin, settling into a semi-vacant chamber in his chest, making itself at home. He lets his arms slide round her and has another moment of flashing realization that he'd never done this in his life before Malaas: just sat and held a woman to his chest, felt the simple joy of that act on a deep and primal level. Now with her, he's done it twice in the same amount of days. He promptly decides that he will do it again as many times as he possibly can.

"I want you to come with me." He says to her, and pulls back so he can look at her face, judge her reaction while simultaneously scanning the entrance to the clearing as he speaks. Supposedly in accordance with edicts handed down all the way from the Central Provinces, the Wah'Ehvi keepers of law long ago branded all unsanctioned fighting completely illegal in Wah'Ehvi Towne, particularly Death Duels, so Kithiik's involvement in the Tunnel Fights has necessitated a certain level of secrecy from a very early age. But for some reason, it seems like a totally different thing to speak as part of a covert group owing its allegiance to a creature he's spent half his lifetime dreaming about killing. Amazing the turns one's life could take, given but the throw of the gods' dice in a particular direction.

"That was part of what Shunkerr had to tell me, more than just about the…cult. I guess She's chosen me for some kind of task that's gonna take me into the Provinces, I don't know what yet."

"Really?" Malaas says, her eyes going a little wide for a second, "I'd love to go with you, wherever she sends you. I haven't left since I was brought to Wah'Ehvi Towne all those cycles ago. This trip to MaahgTain is the furthest I've traveled beyond the town's borders. Perhaps it is time that changes for both of us."

The tension of the preceding moment now completely defused, Kithiik releases a breath of relief, and offers up a silent prayer of thanks to his new gods, those whose names he does not yet know, the ones who've been smiling down upon him since he met a strange, masked healer woman in a fever dream who's turned out to be such a wonderful companion in the real world. Malaas extricates herself from his embrace and stands, stretching in the serpent light, looking relieved and splendid and vital. She smiles down at him. "I have to go aid with the preparations for the return journey down the mountain. I'll see you at the farewell dinner this eve?"

"Yeah, see you then."

She turns to walk away, but not before reaching down to grab the back of his neck and pulling his head up to meet her sumptuous lips in a delicious, lingering kiss that puts a strain on the front of his leggings. He watches the sway of her hips and the delightful jiggle of her round buttocks as she leaves, then goes in search of Nasiya. He hasn't the faintest idea of how to go about finding her but he remembers their guide's exhortation when he first led them down from the plateau. The Ethu told them to ask anyone they encountered whatever questions they might have. Kithiik begins to wander the paths rather aimlessly, with the dim idea that he'll come across an Ethu who can tell him where Nasiya might be found. His wandering takes him past an archway wherein he catches sight of one of the guards Wheirdaahn sat with the night before. Though still considered a youngling by most of them, Kithiik has always found himself at ease in the company of guards and their ilk, particularly those older than twenty-seven cycles or so. Retired soldiers, ex-mercenaries, these men tend toward simple things and simple rules. Respect them and to a degree, most of them will offer the same energy in kind. Fortunately for Kithiik, this guard proves no exception and he saves Kithiik the trouble of having to wander the entire city looking for Nasiya. The guard hails him as he walks up.

"Greetings. You enjoying your sojourn here in our lovely city?"

Kithiik grins at flashed memories of flesh and twined limbs amid spongy, moss-covered walls. "Aye, I am indeed. I have somewhat I would ask of you?"

"What is it you're lookin' for?"

"Would you know where I could find Nasiya, the Ethu girl

___”

"Ha!" The guard guffaws for a moment, interrupting Kithiik and good naturedly slapping him on the back as he does so.

"Of course I know who Nasiya is. No one from round here doesn't. She's a wild one she is, even for an Ethu. Does what she pleases, rest of the world be damned. You gotta little crush, do ya?" He guffaws again at Kithiik's weak protestations about wanting to find her for other reasons and continues speaking.

"Well it's no matter to me why you wish to find her, lad. Last night's was a spectacle like to give many a lad a hankering to find her, I'd think. But you're not from any of the mountain cities are you? You're from down the mountain I'd wager. Either way, I do indeed know where she is most like to be found. All the youngling Ethu girls tend to gather at one place when they're not getting into trouble—which is most of the time I can tell you." The guard grins sagely as he imparts this information, quite obviously enjoying his role as tutor. Kithiik can only imagine the kinds of mischief Ethu girls get into, especially ones with the attitude and bearing of Nasiya.

"It's a spring maybe midway between here and the Globed Towers—you can most likely find Nasiya, and a buncha others besides, resting at the spring. Be warned, boys don't go to Stalkers Spring unless they're lookin' for the best kind of trouble. Don't go anywhere near there if you're in a rush. You won't get where you're goin' anytime soon; I can promise you that. They got a hidin' game they play, all the Ethu seem to play it, young and old, but the youth are all over it, 'specially the ones preparing to leave the city for wandering.

"I swear, if more soldiers played games like that when they were coming up…Anyways, the female younglings practice theirs at the spring, seein' how well hidden they can get in the fastest amount of time, sneakin' up on each other, and anybody else in the vicinity. Once they get their hands on you it's anybody's guess what happens, totally depends on their mood at the time." He winks again. A thought occurs to Kithiik right then, and he jumps on it while he's got the opportunity.

"My thanks for helping me, but there is one more thing while I have your ear: What did you think of what happened last night?"

"You mean before or after the room went crackerbarrels and all serpent shyte broke loose? I couldn't quite tell you, lad. I've lived here for decacycles and there's still things I can't understand for the life of me. Last night was one of those things. I stopped questioning a long time ago—the Ethu are a thauma'd people for sure, and some of it we won't ever be able to fathom. It was tense in there for a time, I know that much." Seeing the obvious interest on Kithiik's face, the guard gives him a little bit more.

"Sometimes being around the Ethu can be like that. You get the feeling you should be grasping something, or seeing something that's right before your face, but you can't see it to save your life. Like I said, I stopped questioning cycles ago. But I think it rubs off on us after a time, I do. You notice strange things you been here long enough. I'm content just to live smack in the middle of it."

Here he pauses for a second, seemingly on the verge of going deeper before he catches himself. "Ahh, anyway, you got a girl to go find, don't ya? Take that path you were on 'til you get to a fork.

Follow the left fork. Don't take any of the paths that lead off it, just keep following it 'til its end. You'll know you're getting close when it starts winding. Good luck, enjoy yourself."

"Again, you have my thanks," Kithiik says to the guard before starting off in the direction he's been given. He walks for a time, making it to the fork and taking the left path. Deeply immersed in pondering the words of the guard and his experience the night before, Kithiik is brought up short by an appreciative whistle the likes of which he'd normally hear in front of a tavern when a pretty girl walks by. He cannot at first locate the source until he hears the whistle again, and he's only slightly surprised when he looks up to discover Nasiya languorously reclining upon a moss-covered tree branch quite a distance above the forest floor, a delightfully wicked smile on her face. Even from so far below her, he fancies he can see the mischief in her eyes.

"I hope you were looking for me cuz I damn sure wanted to be found," she says. "I think I properly thanked you last night. I must've cuz you're back already, but by bark and seed you keep really good company!" Kithiik feels himself grinning like an unfledged academy boy but can't bring himself to stop. "Greetings, Nasiya. Is there someplace we can speak?"
She's out of the tree before he can figure out how she managed it, standing before him like an especially wicked-minded animal. The mischief in her expression doesn't dim in the slightest, nor does her smile waver as she answers him, husky voice lightly teasing.

"Certainly, fine one, I'll take you anywhere you wanna go. You're not about to confess to falling under the spell of my yoni are you? Cuz then I'll have to admit I might of fallen a little bit in love myself with that beautiful cock of yours, sexy boy. I'd jump you right now except I'm still a little sore. You know you've been blessed with a nice, thick, beautiful cock, right? You gave it to me juuust how I like it."

He's sure he'd be beet red if his skin tone permitted. Her audacity is so far beyond his ken he has no answer for it, but he tries anyway, fumbling with his words like a mouthful of hot stones. "I have somewhat… There is something I'd…like to talk to you about before we depart. You know we leave…the caravan, you know we strike out at first light tomorrow morn?" She laughs at his broken speech, his obvious discomfort, and steps close enough to him to set his heart beating double.

"Come with me, beautiful boy," she purrs at him, taking his hand in hers, contriving to brush a hip against the nascent bulge at the front of his breeches. "I've got the perfect place we can… talk." Pulling him off the trail, she runs with him into the forest.

END BOOK 1

GLOSSARY

Astraloger's Guild: Guild where thauma is practiced and taught to novices, adepts, and sensitives as well as the study of light serpent behavior, the glimoreen and their arrangements in the night skocean.

Atro-city: Any of several large-scale, completely enclosed prisons built primarily to house those individuals who have committed the most unforgiveable of crimes, including that of pursuing the advancement of technology

Blade bands: Groups of mercenaries in which each individual has been trained in the use of a specific bladed weapon and has then trained in using his weapons in tandem with all other members of the group. These groups are frequently contracted out as a sort of enforcement arm in addition to the local keepers of law.

Chronicler(s): Jongleurs, itinerant storytellers, wandering bards.

Claahns'Dane (klonz-DANE): Part of the ancestral thauma (magic) of the Ethu, which confers a hereditary war dance upon every full-blooded member of the race.
Elder race: Any of the races present on Eh'Nas before the coming of humankind.

Crimm (krim): The criminal element.

Daughters/Stone Daughters: Blood offspring of the Mistress resulting from her mating with human males.

Delicates: A race of albinos who have become so successful within the Provinces they are considered the unofficial authorities in most every trend, fashion, fad and style among the affluent circles. Second only to the royalty in status, they enjoy a sort of celebrity amongst the Provinces.

Domina/Domineh (DOME-ee-nuh/DOME-ee-nay- female/male respectively): A title for the dominant partner in relationships with a very specific dynamic on Eh'Nas; Additionally a way of referring to any individual who inherently leans toward the dominant side of the paradigm versus the submissive side.

Ethu (AYE-thoo or EE-thoo): An elder race, very like humans but different in several aspects. Because of the length of their ears and the extreme white pigment of their skin, it is speculated that they may have descended from the elves of human legend, but no one can attest to the truth of this.

Ethu Thone (AYE-thoo th•OWN): The most warlike and battle-hungry clan of Ethu ever to walk the forests of the TlammaTain mountain range.

Float water: Water from any of several floating lakes situated throughout Eh'Nas. Because of the mineral-rich content of the waters and their curious side effect of being a naturally mild intoxicant, drinks made from the water and the water itself have come to be highly valued all over the Provinces.

Gypsy city: One of several mysterious small trading/merchant/bazaar cities that appear at the beginning of snakeset and disappear just before snakerise in random places throughout the Provinces and beyond. No one knows where they come from or how many there are because it's impossible to count them and one can never be sure if it's the same city or a slightly different one as they all appear markedly similar.

Gravity 'pents/gravity serpents: It is said that the gravity in the land of **Eh'Nas** (aye-NAHS) is created by gigantic serpents deep beneath the surface of the ground coiled together in huge, living knots and spinning incessantly. It is the spinning that creates the gravity. It is thought that the largest of these living knots lies at the very center of the world.

Keepers of the clocks: The office of those whose job it is to keep time in the various provinces and city towns prosperous enough in trade to need to deal with exact time. Clock keepers set the time for the clocks in a particular region and thus, the time for every province is different. Things can become doubly confusing during and after Sa'aeon because of the incredible irregularity of the light serpents during this time. As such, Sa'aeon has been designated the official celebration season for all of Eh'Nas, a monthlong holiday where official time is suspended and fetes last for days and nights on end.

Keepers of law: Police officers charged by the governing bodies of the Provinces with keeping the peace and enforcing local law within them.

Light serpents: The land of Eh'Nas has no sun. Instead, extremely bright, gargantuan flying serpents composed of living light provide copious amounts of illumination during the day. These creatures travel in groups called pods. Local time is largely measured by the crossings of three major serpent pods across the skocean. Hence, the dawn pod or first crossing, the midday pod or second crossing, and the evening pod or third crossing.

MaahgTain (Mog-Tane): An alpine city located at a precipitous altitude in the TlammaTain mountains situated on a plateau between two of the Three Peaks. It was founded by the first interspecies coupling between a human, in this case Maahg the Second, and an Ethu, a female called Thairn.

MaahgThairn (Mog-TARN): The floating lake that keeps fully half the mountain kingdom of

MaahgTain in its shadow. It floats above the city but well below the skocean above it.

The lake is named for an Ethu female named Thairn. Maahg the Second fell in love with her and founded the city upon the spot where they first consummated their union. But although she would go on to rule alongside him, she perpetually refused to marry him, saying that no Ethu woman would be tamed by the rules and walls of men. He named the floating lake after her because she remained, like the lake, perpetually present but eternally floating just out of reach.

Memory delvers: A class of adepts who use their thauma to journey through a person's heritage, accessing the abilities, talents and skillstheir ancestors and ancient ancestors once possessed and bringing knowledge of those skills back to the present.

Naatchri luunpha (NOT-tree LOON-fah): Nature magic, the first half of the ancestral thauma of the Ethu, which gives them a deep connection with nature and preternatural abilities with growing things.

Namash (nah-MOSH): The medicine people of the Ethu.

Nagraj (nah-GRRAHZH [with a rolled r]): Within the cult of the Serpentari, any male who has survived the Venemaste with his wits intact goes on to become Nagraj, a male worthy of being consort to the Mistress and/or her daughters.

Night bells: Official time in the Provinces is kept by the keepers of the clocks, and broken down into two halves, eight bells during the day and another eight at night.

Peeress Chosen: The title bestowed by the Mistress upon a male who survives the Venemaste and, as such, comes under her especial protection.

Pent maps/serpent charts: Maps made by the astraloger guilds in every city, town and province that chart the movements and seasonal behavioral patterns of light serpent pods over given regions. Travelers use the maps to navigate as they travel and to plan their trips.

Rawks: Large, relatively slow-moving, three-horned bovines used primarily as pack animals but also as a source of leather and meat by certain peoples. These creatures look like a weird cross between a robust variety of cow and a sheep.

Renewal Pilgrims: At the end of Sa'aeon, when the mating season for the light serpents is over, the days return to normal. This point is called the Renewal, and Renewal Pilgrims come from all over Eh'Nas to witness the light serpents' return to their normal flights across the skocean.

Sa'aeon (sah-EE-ahn): Shortest of the three seasons, it lasts only a single month but is the most intense of the three because it is the mating season of the light serpents and thus is generally accompanied by the strangest weather and the weirdest happenings. For most of Eh'Nas, Sa'aeon has been officially declared the holiday/festival season.

Sensitive: One who is born with an extra affinity for working with and/or sensing thauma.

Skocean (SKO-shun): Commonly used abbreviation for sky ocean, referring to the fact that the sky above all of Eh'Nas is literally an ocean.

Snakerise/snakeset: The moment the light serpents rise above the horizon, and when they sink below it, bringing the light and taking it with them.

[The] Stone Garden: name of a cult within a cult. Human females trained in secret by the Stone Daughters. Most live otherwise normal lives, waiting for the moment when they are summoned for whatever the Mistress ultimately has in mind for them.

Thauma/mahj'ick (th-OW-muh/mah-JEEK): Magic and/or the preternatural forces that exist just outside our perception, many of which may be sensed, manipulated, communicated with or otherwise harnessed in specific ways under specific circumstances by those with either a learned or intuitive knowledge of how to access them.

The Three Peaks: Tlamm Hurr (tlom-HER), Tlamm Uute (tlom-OOT) and Tlamm Rem (tlom-REM). Tlamm Rem is known as one of the "Supreme Peaks" because it reaches so high it goes right up and through the skocean.

TrueStyle lore: The knowledge passed on from one Ethu keeper to the next of the original Claahns'Dane of an individual clan.

Twaesting (TWAY-sting): The harnessing or manipulation of thauma for a specific purpose or to gain a particular result. A spell.

The Under: A catchall term to roughly describe the underbelly of any given place, particularly urban centers, and a sense of the energy that accompanies and embodies that underbelly.

Venemaste (ven-uh-MAHS-tay): The Ordeal by Poison, a process through which the Mistress determines, by poisoning them during copulation, which human males are worthy to be her consorts.

Wah'Ehvi House (wah-EH-vee): A very successful wine and liqueur company founded by Reshu Wah'Ehvi and run by he and his son. The company eventually grew so large, the people of the little hamlet it was based in renamed the town after them.

Afterword

Hello you human reading this. First and foremost, I would really just like to say thank you for getting this far, and for taking this ride.

I have been an avid reader of sci-fi/fantasy forever. And just as long, I've frequently found myself wondering why, if this was supposed to be fantasy and new worlds/alternative realities, did I continue to see the exact same gender, power, and sexual dynamics playing out over and over again? Where were the heroes/heroines of alternative gender and ethnic heritage and above and beyond all of that, where was all the sex?! I've read countless pages of violent, line-by-line descriptions of bloody warfare and enchanted blades wreaking havoc, but in almost every case, I'd be fortunate to get a fraction of a paragraph about someone's flesh being pleasured. What is that all about?

I hope you are satisfied with this first foray, and that you are sufficiently titillated to come along for the rest of the ride. I will try my best not to disappoint you.

By way of a ps: I would love to hear back from you about your experience of this book! Honest feedback is extremely appreciated. I mean that [so long as it's constructive. I am at least partially human and I DO have feelings!] Please, if you feel so moved, tell a friend about it, put up a review someplace; buy one [or several] as gifts!
Just a thought… {smiling}

If You Enjoyed This Ride, Don't Forget To Check Out The Next
Books In This Salacious Series!

CULT OF THE SERPENTARI: TABOO RITES, BOOK 2
CULT OF THE SERPENTARI: TABOO RITES, BOOK 3

http://artofmicah.com/product

A Bit About ME [Micah BlackLight]

I am here to create the most brilliant, evocative, challenging, innovative, impact I am capable of, to have THE most fun while doing it, and to leave a trail of empowering, inspiring interactions in my wake like a spirit boat traveling this lake of existence.

Unmarried husband, dedicated father, poet, artist, illustrator, writer, author, Empowerment coach, couture fashion designer, self-proclaimed badass and maker of badassery.
Statistic defy-er, loving, accepting,
understanding, perceptive HUMAN
BEING. I am a fire tender and dream
holder and secret keeper.
I am a poem disguised as a song masquerading as a human
being and clothed in the flesh of a brown male.
I am unbowed and unbroken.
I am whole without my mate, and part of a WHOOLE other
whole with her. I am the breaking of my dysfunctional familial
patterns embodied.
I am power jacked into the cockpit of my flesh.
I am ALIVE and an ever-beacon for those who need an example
of how it can look to BLAZE as a self- expressed being, giving
others whatever permission they need to declare THEMSELVES
Badass in turn.
I, like every single one of you, am a dream of my ancestors
embodied.
We are the future of a past long buried.
We are potential made manifest
and I will continue for so long as I am able
to be an Inspiration ENGINE,
a soul screamer

a permanent and most eloquent reminder of magic,
BLAZING the truth of me in the faces of those who do not believe
that people like us *EXIST*
I am reflection and mirror and mirrored.
I am swimming in Gratitude Lake.
I am love
And sending love
To You.
(Yes, YOU!)

artofmicah.com